A
DARKLY
BEATING
HEART

Also by Lindsay Smith

Sekret
Skandal
Dreamstrider

A DARKLY BEATING HEART

LINDSAY SMITH

ROARING BROOK PRESS
NEW YORK

Library of Congress Control Number: 2016932186

ISBN 978-1-62672-044-2

Our books may be purchased in bulk for promotional, educational, or business use. Please contact your local bookseller or the Macmillan Corporate and Premium Sales Department at (800) 221-7945 ext. 5442 or by e-mail at MacmillanSpecialMarkets@macmillan.com.

First edition 2016
Book design by Elizabeth H. Clark
Printed in the United States of America

1 3 5 7 9 10 8 6 4 2

For Ashlan

風をいたみ
岩うつ波の
おのれのみ
くだけて物を
思ふ頃かな

❖

"Like a driven wave,
Dashed by fierce winds on a rock,
So am I: alone
And crushed upon the shore,
Remembering what has been."

—Minamoto no Shigeyuki
(13th century)

CHAPTER ONE

UNCLE SATORI SAYS MASTERY IS A WELL-WORN PATH.
(At least, that's how my cousin Akiko translated it for me, though I rarely take her at her word.) If he's right, then I am mastering a path of hatred, carving it deeper every day like the scars along my thighs. I wake up with a hatred that gnaws at me like hunger, and I feed that hatred with Akiko's snores from the other side of the room. I feed it with the sight of my megalith suitcase spewed open beside my pallet, still not unpacked. And with the one unread email clogging my phone's notifications that I can't bring myself to read.

If I carve a path deep enough, then it will become a trench. A grave. Carve it deep enough, and I'll never have to climb out.

In the three months since I arrived in Tokyo, I've made a

routine that turns me inside out with exhaustion and keeps my thoughts on their well-worn trail. That's what I came here for—a distraction, something to overload my senses and leave me to my self-devouring mind. No time to think about what came before or whatever might come next. Maybe my parents hoped I'd learn mindfulness here, or obedience, or drive, or at least a goddamned Japanese phrase or two beyond *sumimasen—excuse me, forgive me, please pardon me for all the evil I've done.* But no, all I've accomplished is that I've filtered my raw hate into something potent, clarified, lethal.

I have mastered the path of hatred, and I know now where it ends.

It ends with my revenge.

❖

I leave Uncle Satori's apartment with my anger burning through me like a grease fire. The sidewalks of Shinjuku are clean as ever: gray asphalt and crisp white lines and slender concrete fingers of apartment buildings thrust toward a crystal blue sky. Nothing like Seattle, where we smear our lives and our insides across every surface—yarn bombs knitted around statues and trees and signs, used chewing gum crusted against the Market Theater wall, ripe with our saliva and germs. I think that's what my parents have never understood about our life in America: that we're not meant to keep everything locked inside, preserving a uniform façade for everyone else's benefit. Hideki and I lived our lives in a kind of purgatory, halfway between our parents' stonewalled world and the wild, free-range one our classmates inhabited, never able to stretch out fully in either one.

I feed two 100-yen coins into a vending machine and crack open a hot can of Suntory Boss coffee (*the boss of them all*, I say to myself). Black-clad office workers in modest heels and starched white button-downs join me in an eerie, silent parade—our daily mourning processional. Right on cue, I see my favorite couple, husband and wife, walking side by side, not speaking, not making eye contact, and when we reach the corner, her hand darts toward his for a hasty squeeze before he turns the corner without a word.

I want to scream at them—interrupt our vow of silence. *So do it*, I imagine Chloe would tell me. *Disrupt the status quo. Break free and make everyone know your name.*

But it's not yet time. When I get the guts to do it, it's her name everyone will know. She'll be the one to take the blame.

In the subway station, the train arrives with a polite ding. I've fantasized before about flinging myself in front of it, too fast for the white-gloved train pushers to catch. Clog up a million salarymen's morning commutes. But it's useless to throw myself in front of a train as it pulls into the station, as I've learned from my extensive research. The train's already decelerating, and a lot of cities use recessed track wells so the average would-be suicide usually survives, albeit with grievous body blows and broken bones. Anyway, I didn't come here with suicide in mind, though if it serves my goal, I won't dismiss it. These fantasies, for now, are part of the dark need for vengeance beating inside of me. My death has to serve a purpose—make someone else suffer even more.

We all shuffle on, sucked inside like the pristine cars are a massive set of lungs. "Please take care that your typing sounds do not disturb other passengers," the signs implore. I know my black metal playlist is seeping out of my cheap earbuds, but I don't care. The other passengers look away, look down, look anywhere but at me.

I close my eyes and sink into the dark forests and ghost-filled castles of the black metal songs as though they're a sludge, pulling me under. This playlist is all Chloe—it keeps my wounds nice and raw. One night in the summer camp art studios, when we'd been painting our canvases and each other, she snatched my phone to get us some music and declared my half-assed collection of '70s soft rock and classical piano sonatas to be an unmatched tragedy. "Let me fix this for you," she said. I think part of me believed she meant my life. She taught me how to kiss to the aching chords of Opeth and the thrashing drums of Cannibal Corpse and Sleater-Kinney's refined rage.

It's been over a year now since she chewed me up and spit me out. A year since I was dumb enough to believe that she (or anyone) could love a fucked-up, forgettable little girl like me. For ten short weeks at the PNW Summer Arts Camp, I was cool. I was hot. I wasn't Saint Isaac's Preparatory Academy's punch line and punching bag. She showed me that all the tangled-up feelings I had for other humans didn't have to stay inside my head. That I could trail love on her skin and smear hate on the canvas in a vicious dance, hot and cold.

The playlist starts over again. The trains get more crowded as we draw closer to the center of Tokyo: schoolgirls in uniform, holding down their pleated skirts to defend against perverts with camera phones, elderly women in quilt coats with bags of groceries, sneer-lipped kids my age punching away at their (respectfully silenced) handheld game consoles.

After Chloe released my carefully maintained feelings, I left camp and returned home to start school, locking them away again. But I didn't forget that summer before my senior year when I was free. And so when we had our first long weekend in the fall, I hopped a bus down to Portland to see her. Her new girlfriend answered the door.

That's when my Chloe problem really began.

I exit the Shibuya station onto the dense neon hub of iconic

Tokyo. Maid cafés, hyperactive fashion shops, pachinko parlors, karaoke bars, and all the latest electronics advertised on retina-scorching five-story screens, with the scent of Asahi beer and boiling ramen stock drifting over it all. Shibuya is what Westerners think when they think of modern Japan. It's bright, it's shiny, but still there's a scrim of silence laid over everything (the slot machine parlors blaring J-pop being the sole exception) and order, always order, even in the platform vinyl boots and gaunt *ikemen* cute boys. I reach the epicenter, the Shibuya scramble crosswalk, where a dozen peninsulas meet, crammed with pedestrians all waiting for traffic to stop so they can cross at once.

I plow my way through the orderly lines of pedestrians the moment the light turns. Maybe someday the streetlights will malfunction, and all the intersecting streets will be green at once and everyone will get crushed in the center of colliding cars.

I reach Satori Graphics, 4F, as the sign reads in front of the narrow concrete building. Nominally, I work in my uncle's design firm. The job was part of my parents' stipulation for allowing me to defer college to go "find myself" or "wait for a spot on Rhode Island School of Design's wait list to open up" or whatever lame excuse I used. None of the explanations mention what happened to Hideki—the real reason they let me come to Japan at all.

It's a small business, fewer than thirty employees, and we mainly design websites, catalogs, fliers, menus, and signs for other small businesses around Tokyo. Mostly, though, it seems to serve as a halfway house for weirdo creative types who couldn't hack it on Japan's notoriously brutal high school and college exams or refused the typical salaryman work-as-life system.

I'm a "layout assistant" since I've refused to do serious artwork after what happened with Chloe. I place all the non-text graphical elements that Kenji, our junior illustrator, designs, then Mariko, the junior copywriter, fills in the Japanese because I've still barely learned a handful of Japanese characters. My cousin Akiko, who merits her own office because she's the owner's daughter, works as our junior team's "project assistant." Apparently that means her job is to nag the rest of us while she browses fashion sites, manages her not-so-budding J-pop lifestyle empire, or sneaks off with her boyfriend.

"Good morning, Reiko." Kenji peers around his monitor as I flop into my desk chair. "Mm, I take it you beat Aki out the door again," he says in English, then drums the butt of a black Sharpie against his lips.

"You know how she needs her beauty rest. Gotta snag her shooting star," I say. But the little wrinkle appears between his eyebrows, underneath a fan of black bangs, that always shows up when he doesn't understand. "Rising star," I say. "Because she wants to be a pop star—"

"Right, right." His face eases back into its usual soft smile before he disappears back behind his monitor. "I thought you

7

meant . . . mm . . . never mind." He pops the cap off of his Sharpie and resumes drawing on a wooden scrap.

Never mind. Everyone's favorite euphemism for "it's too much effort to try to put it in English for you." Which is everyone's favorite euphemism for "I can't believe you've been here four months and still haven't learned more than a few phrases." I gesture to his piece of wood. "What're you working on?" I ask him. "Some sort of viral marketing campaign?"

Kenji pauses; the slender bones of his hand tighten. "Mm . . ." He flips the piece toward him, hesitant, but then he extends it underneath our monitors toward me. "It's an *ema*. A prayer board. You write your wishes on it and hang it up at a Shinto shrine."

I glance at his precise columns of writing on one side, then flip it over to the other side. The *ema* is triangular, and Kenji's used the shape to draw an elaborate wolfish head on the back. He's a great artist—quick and precise in his work for Satori Design—but here, he's showing a completely new style. It's not just some cartoon corgi promoting a WiFi subscription or a cartoon bunny shilling a sale on dishwashing detergent. These prayers clearly mean a great deal to him.

Another kindling on the pyre of my hatred: people who are still capable of believing. In anything.

"I didn't know you were religious," I say, too casually, as I hand the *ema* back.

Kenji slips it into the breast pocket of his gray-and-black

plaid shirt. "Shinto isn't really—religion, you know. You don't have to get the thing with the water on the head, any of that."

"Baptized."

"Right, that," Kenji says. "Visiting shrines and all, it's a tradition. I do it every week."

Like Saint Isaac's, with their weekly assemblies in the smaller chapel of Saint Isaac's Prep. I remember one assembly in particular. Me standing in the front, tears blurring my sight as I read the court-ordered apology. *I have come before you all today to beseech you for your forgiveness. I've sinned not only against God, but against each and every one of you . . .*

"Shinto's just how I grew up. If something's bothering me, or I'm hoping for something, then I go to the shrine and let go of those fears or hopes, whatever emotion it is, give it over to the spirits." He smiles that self-effacing grin that folds shyly back on itself. "Then I can get on with whatever I need to do."

What he needs to do. I've been carving my routine deeper every day, but I'm not making any progress on what I need to do. I need payback against Chloe, against Hideki, against my parents, even against Akiko. Hideki showed me I have to be sure I go far enough. I want a trail of scorched earth in my wake.

"Sounds great," I tell him. But I have my own work to prepare. It's like an itch, burning beneath my skin. I duck my head behind the monitor and carve the path of vengeance a little deeper into my mind.

Akiko staggers in twenty minutes before lunch, comically large sunglasses concealing her hangover eyes. Kenji hurriedly chucks the manga he'd been reading into his bag, and I let my boots slip off the edge of the desk. As usual, she's dressed up for the red carpet, not for another day at the office: fur-trimmed jacket, embroidered skinny jeans, platform boots that ensure she'll tower over the rest of us, and her lightened brown hair set in ringlets that bounce in time with her steps. We're not her intended audience, though—that honor goes to Tadashi, her helicopter boyfriend, and whatever entertainment industry suit he's bribing to invest in the aki * LIFE * rhythm brand.

She says something in Japanese, nothing I understand, but Kenji, Mariko, and Kazuo, a junior sales rep, bob their heads with varying levels of enthusiasm and mutter a few *hai*s of compliance. Then Akiko turns to me and smiles, a vulpine look. "Reiko, I know you are not clever enough to have learned Japanese still, but I was just telling the others that we're going to lunch together today." She pauses to take a sip of coffee. "I have a big announcement to make."

A big announcement. Just what I want to hear. I yank my long black hair into a sloppy ponytail and follow my co-workers back out to Shibuya. Mariko whines that we haven't gone to the pancake café recently, but we find ourselves at the usual *ramen-ya*. We order at a vending machine at the front of the restaurant: just insert your money and punch the button with the photograph of the soup you want.

We scoot past the row of salarymen in matching suits, all facing the wall like naughty schoolchildren while they slurp their ramen. Mariko slides first into the booth, then Aki heaps her jacket and purse on Mariko, who scrambles to fold them and stack them neatly beside her. I slide onto the bench opposite Mariko. Kazuo slides in next to me, eyes never once lifting from his PlayStation Vita handheld console. I catch a glimpse of a busty sorceress charging a skeletal dragonlord on the Vita's screen. Kenji squeezes in on Kazuo's other side.

"I've landed a job," Aki says, then says it again, louder, when no one responds. "I've landed a job performing at the Kuramagi Cultural Festival. And you're all going to go with me."

Kuramagi. Where's Kuramagi? The others are offering half-hearted congratulations in Japanese, but my pounding pulse fills my ears. I don't want to leave Tokyo. This is where I've mastered my path.

The waitress arrives and drops bowls of ramen down the length of the table, then passes a tray of *gyoza*, fried pork potstickers, toward Mariko. Aki arches one brow. "Oh," Aki says, "I didn't know you were eating things like that again."

Mariko's teeth catch the collar of her jacket and her head shrinks back, her pudgy cheeks shining with red.

"Anyway, this is a huge opportunity for the aki * LIFE *

rhythm empire. I will need everyone's help to make the festival a success. Kazuo?"

Huge opportunity. No. I can't leave. I can't break out of my routine. I squeeze my chopsticks so hard they break.

But they're paying me no mind. Kazuo snaps at Akiko in Japanese, and Mariko giggles, once, into her jacket collar. I start to grin, drawn to their discord like it's blood in the water. If I can get them fighting with each other, then maybe we won't have to leave.

But Akiko's hand shoots across the table in a flurry of lacquered nails and seizes his handheld game. She dangles it right over her deep bowl of ramen. Kazuo cries out, and the sorceress bounces up and down on the screen, her tinny moans thick as the rising steam in the dead silence of our table.

"I need you all to understand that this is a team effort. When we are in my father's office, we are a team focused on the task of creating excellent graphics for his clients. But when you are with me, we are focused on the sole task of building my fan base. We are launching my career. *Our* careers. Even simple Reiko's. Do not forget that I'm doing this for all of us."

All of us. Another lie. We're playing her media team for extra spending money. She's playing pop star, vlogger, and dispenser of advice on fashion, love, and other topics for which she has zero qualification. Not only do I hate people who believe in things and care about things, but I especially hate people who have a high regard for themselves. And dare to think that others should care about them, too.

"To be fair," Kenji says, gesturing with his chopsticks, "we've only seen a fraction of the money you've promised us."

Akiko flings Kazuo's Vita back at him. "And whose fault do you suppose that is?"

Kenji shrugs. "My portraits of you are selling pretty well on the e-store."

"My posts on your Mixi profile get a lot of likes," Mariko says.

"Then you're—*Reiko*! What's the phrase?" Aki snaps her fingers at me. "When he's tugging himself. No, pulling himself."

"Ah," I stammer, "I don't . . ." My head feels scrambled. I was going to plan something here—in Tokyo. I don't want to be ripped away.

"Come on, keep up!" Aki snaps her fingers in front of my face. "Kenji is pulling—"

"Pulling his weight." I manage to break through the fog and find my way back to my path. I don't understand why we need to leave Tokyo.

"Yes. You're pulling your weight. Everyone else—"

"'Sup, *otaku*?" Tadashi sways up to our table. Akiko's talent manager-slash-sort-of-boyfriend never seems to lack funds to buy those shiny skinny jeans and shades and bleached-tip haircuts, but still mooches off the rest of us when we go out. He grabs a dumpling off Mariko's tray, pops it in his mouth, and perches on the edge of the bench next to Akiko, stroking the bleached goatee that drapes his face like a bad taxidermy job. "Aki. Baby. Who loves you?"

Aki snaps her chopsticks apart with a sound like gunfire. "I hope you have more good news for me."

"*aidoruLOVE* magazine is sending a journalist to report on hot new trends at the Kuramagi Cultural Festival." Tadashi couldn't look more pleased with himself if he'd turned our broth into liquid gold.

Aki juts her chin toward him, like she's expecting more. "And?"

"And? And I'm gonna try to get them to write a feature on you." He grins. "Duh."

"But they haven't agreed to it yet," Aki says.

Tadashi plucks the pickled egg out of Aki's ramen. "They will," he says, custardy yolk oozing into his whiskers.

"Kazuo," she says, "I need website updates. New sections. A feed of all the good press aki * LIFE * rhythm is getting."

"Yup. I'll code it later." Kazuo runs one hand through his stubby fauxhawk while he plays.

"And Reiko," Aki's devious smile turns on me, "historic photo shoots for the historic village. Make it happen."

I stare back at her. What the fuck am I supposed to know about Japanese history? How am I supposed to arrange

14

costumes or anything in a strange village when I can barely say *sumimasen*? I stare into my bowl.

Kenji taps my shin under the table. "I'll contact a kimono rental company," he says. "Just worry about lighting and so on."

His voice is kind, but it makes my insides convulse. "Okay. Sure."

I don't look up. The Reiko of a year ago would have devoured the glistening, tender pork cutlets and perfectly seasoned broth in three gulps, but I feel too wrung out and shrunken to even try now. I watch the steam wisp and curl through the air while Akiko chatters about plans for our weekend in Kuramagi village. The boys slurp down every last noodle of their ramen. Even Mariko valiantly manages to eat half her bowl, and Akiko sips at the broth. Tadashi slips the untouched *gyoza* in his pockets as we depart.

"You look shaken," Kenji says to me, as we walk back to work.

I shrink into the hood of my jacket. "Why do we have to go to some backwater village?"

"What, the trip to Kuramagi?" His expression softens. "It pays the bills. Should be a pretty village, too. They've preserved all the original Edo-period structures and everything."

I tighten my grip around my satchel and hurry my pace. I don't know what to expect in Kuramagi. I don't have a plan for what to do with my time, my thoughts. And when I don't have a plan, the feelings—the anger—find their way back in.

I rush to the toilet and lock myself in. The programmable electronic toilet seat is sweltering hot against my thighs; someone left it set at max heat. As soon as I lean back, the toilet control panel speakers blast the sounds of rushing water right into my eardrums. Not my favorite conditions, but Akiko's news forced me off my path, and I need to shepherd myself back on course. Everything's been shattered since Hideki's terrible act, and the only thing left is to shatter it more.

Before Hideki left for the medical corps, I'd already mastered the path of secrets, the trick of coiling them up tighter than a nautilus shell. There was always room for more secrets in the black hole of my soul. Crush them all down, make geological layers of them, but never let them see the light of day.

I study the bruises along my wrists and arms—those are from Hideki. But the thin parallel rows of scars along my thighs belong to me.

This hatred belongs to me. Chloe and Hideki and Akiko and my parents and the entire student body of Saint Isaac's Prep can never take it from me. Only I have earned that right. *I am mastering the path of hatred.* The first slice runs only a fraction higher than my oldest scar, my favorite scar, the uneven one wrought by an unsteady hand. The scar of a girl who hadn't yet learned how to unleash the violence that pumped through her heart. The blood wells up sluggishly, thick and already congealing, but the sting is what I crave. The sting of air on all the exposed pain rings clear and perfect through my hollow body.

I am in control. The next slice, right on top of the scar from the day Chloe ruined everything. The day those awful, bloody secrets were bared for all to see. But this blood is for me alone. No one else can see these scars, this smear of red on my shriveled-up thigh. And no one ever will.

The third slice—never more than three, never too deep, never too close together—goes on the other thigh, somewhere in between a scar from Hideki's cruelty and a scar from Hideki's failure. I slump back and let the wave of pain roll through me, loud as the tinny trickling sounds on the toilet speaker box.

I will make them pay.

CHAPTER TWO

AKI THRUSTS ANOTHER CELL PHONE AT ME. "PHOTO,"
she snaps.

I take a step back and sigh. This has been my Sunday so
far—photographing her with tourists at the cosplay gathering grounds of the Jingu-mae bridge in Harajuku. We're
crammed in here with Gothic Lolitas and sword-wielding
Sephiroths and man-eating Titans and Malice Mizers, but she
clears a space and strikes a perfect *kawaii* pose next to the pim-
ply white American tourist: head cocked, one leg kicked back,
two fingers spread wide in victory. "Say *kawaii!*" she hisses
through a clenched-teeth smile, and the guy eagerly obliges.

I snap the photo and exit out to his phone's home screen,
then immediately wish I hadn't—two plump cel-shaded

anime breasts glare out at me from between the app icons. I all but toss the phone at him while Aki does her best to pretend she doesn't understand his declarations of love.

It's our last day in Tokyo, and Aki's making me spend it in the Harajuku district to drum up free publicity for aki * LIFE * rhythm and her performance at the festival. "Tune in on NHK5 to see the big show!" she cheers in English between each song.

Tadashi keeps wandering off to answer his phone, Mariko's already camped out at our usual table at the nearby pancake-serving bunny café, and Kenji's tucked himself into the narrowest corner he can find to sketch the crowd.

And me—I'm playing Aki's photographer even though I hate her frilly candy-blue maid costume and curly caramel-colored hair. But most of all I hate this camera. There was a time when you couldn't pry the camera out of my hand, or the scissors I used to chop up my photos to make collages. But that time feels like a movie I watched long ago, falling asleep during all the good parts. A life that happened to someone else.

"And who are you supposed to be playing, my fair maiden?" The same guy is behind me now, smoothing the front of his silk-print dragon shirt. "No, let me guess. Is it Mako Mori from *Pacific Rim*? You'd look positively ravishing with a touch of blue in your hair." He starts to reach for a lock. "Want to find out if we're drift compatible?"

I jerk violently away from him. I'm shaking with disgust. He thinks he can speak so lewdly to me, that I exist for his adoration. These are the moments when I wish I knew just how to wield all my hatred. But I'm not prepared. No snappy rejoinders at the ready.

"I will carve your insides out," I manage, my voice breaking as I say it. But even then, I only think of it because Chloe once hissed it at some woman on a camp field trip who acted disgusted to see us holding hands. Stupid. Stupid. Now Chloe's back inside my head, her grating laugh, the cocksure way she wrapped my hand around the paintbrush and told me not to hold back.

The guy's stammering out a response, but I'm just thinking of Chloe's words about justice and freedom that always left me hungering for more. I walk away as Aki yells for me, but I ignore her and push through the sea of plastic claymores and wigs like exotic birds.

"Why do you let them call you names?" Chloe had asked, after I told her about Saint Isaac's one late night at camp. How they toss slurs my way, gross Orientalist comments. "You can't let them say that shit to you. They think they won't have to pay? You're an artist. You have power. This is your chance to take control."

So I cut the head off another photograph of a student in a white-and-navy uniform. I painted the cathedral weeping with blood. I don't even remember how the other collage elements got introduced—the guns, the guillotines, the gas masks, and mushroom clouds.

Subversive, Chloe said, standing back, looking at the carnage I'd wrought across the painting studio.

Disruptive, she said, as her arms found my waist.

I had been so sure she was right. That this was what real art was—not the silly elven princesses I'd drawn before, or photos I'd taken of my brother, his combat-haunted smile strained to breaking point. Art was violent and aggressive and charged. Art would set me free.

"Hey, Rei." I'm heading across the bridge, into Yoyogi Park, and Kenji is calling my name, just loud enough for me to hear.

I start to walk past him, pretending not to notice, but guilt tugs me back and I turn toward his bench. "Hi." I jam my fists into the pouch of my hoodie and watch his hands work.

It's a sketch of the chaotic scene on the bridge, of course, but everything's all inverted. The cosplayers and tourists and fashionistas in all their garish glory—they're just background noise, a dull sea of gray. At the center, a skeletal girl with a sloppy braid stands, shoulders back, stance wide. Leather bracelets scale both of her forearms. Ones that perfectly match the ones I'm wearing now.

I look from the drawing toward Kenji's face. He's so intent, and he has these beautiful dark lashes framing his eyes, and the sloppy hair and wry wit and kindness, but . . . I can't do this now. The antidepressants have chiseled away all semblance of a libido from me, and after Chloe, I don't know if I can bear to be touched by anyone ever again. I squeeze my eyes shut and rock back on my heels.

Kenji glances up at me, and his face darkens. "Sorry. I don't mean to be, mm, creepy. I just . . ." He twiddles the pencil between his fingers. "It's practice. For the comic I want to draw."

"What, and she's your main character?" I start to roll my eyes, but manage to stop myself in time. He doesn't deserve that. Of all of our team, he's the one who doesn't deserve to be hurt.

"Maybe." One corner of his mouth twitches into a grin. "I'm still figuring out her backstory." His gaze darts up at me, flashing like fish scales, before sinking again. "What her secret powers are."

I sink onto the bench beside him. "Pretty sure she doesn't have any."

He shrugs and keeps drawing. We sit in companionable silence—I'd forgotten such a thing exists. Usually silence claws at me like a cornered animal, desperate for something to relieve the agony of everything going unsaid. I turn on my camera and snap a shot of Kenji working—it only seems fair, after all, to take his picture when he's drawing me.

"Hey, nerds!" Tadashi calls, striding toward us as he shoves his phone into the back pocket of his jeans. "Kenji. My man." He claps Kenji on the shoulder so hard it jostles both of us, then leans in and whispers something to him in Japanese. Kenji tightens on himself like a fist and shuts his eyes.

Then Tadashi rounds on me. "Rei-rei. Time for Aki to sing, don't you think? Present our *ninkai nanba wan* star! Get some snaps! Help me work the crowd!" He pushes his fingers through the stiff peaks of his frosted bangs, then bounces off to boss around his equipment flunkies who are hauling amplifiers and synth boxes through the crowd.

"And that's my cue to go." I stand up and shake the concrete dust off the butt of my jeans. God, how are they so baggy on me now? They used to call me a pork dumpling back at Saint Isaac's. I wish I could feel proud of myself for shedding the weight, but it's just a side effect of my failed efforts to disappear.

"Not going to get more pictures for Aki's portfolio?" Kenji asks, a teasing grin in his tone.

I roll my eyes. "I've got enough. See you at the café, or something."

"Or something," he echoes. "Yeah."

I stroll along the pathway deeper into Yoyogi Park just as the frenetic strains of some technopop song blasts out of Aki's amplifier. The same song I've heard her practice ad nauseum at the apartment.

The crowds have dried up this far into the wooded park;

the clattering JapanRail trains and honking cars are reduced to nothing but a dull throb behind my eyes. The leaves are still mostly green in Yoyogi, though the overcast sky muffles everything with a gray filter, sapping away the color and life. No birds. No people. Nothing but the dim rustle of branches in the wind. Total, solitary silence. I hate it and love it—love that I have space to breathe and think, hate the thoughts that take the opportunity to crowd into my head.

I pass under a hulking wooden *torii*, the Japanese-style archway that marks the winding path toward Emperor Meiji's shrine. Massive wooden racks holding sake barrels, wine, beer, and countless other offerings from around the world line the path. Emperor Meiji is a Shinto spirit now, because he ended the centuries of military shogun leadership and brought Japan into the modern era, which apparently meant opening it up to Western influence. Doesn't sound like that great of a deal to me, but now Emperor Meiji gets to hang out with all the other spirits and drink sake and party all the time until someone petitions him with a prayer, like Kenji with his *ema* board.

I reach the main area of the shrine. The slate square, hemmed in by a variety of wooden structures with weathered green roofs, is empty save for a white-swathed Shinto priest meticulously sweeping the stones. A breeze snakes through the square, rattling the *ema* boards that dangle from the prayer wall and swirling dead leaves around my legs. The priest pauses, glancing up at me with a tiny frown before he returns to his work. I wrap my arms around my chest and shuffle deeper into the temple grounds.

I'm lost in my own homeland, ignorant of my own language, my culture, my customs, my heritage. I had to plead with my parents to send me here, revisit their birth land, or at least, that's the excuse I used. They preferred to keep their heritage like a coffee table book to display at parties, not anything to look too closely at. The tech industry was their tribe, and Saint Isaac's their religion. Their children were a newly compiled source code in constant need of upgrades. When Hideki went to Stanford, my parents were sure, so sure, at least one of them had served their purpose. And for a time, I Hideki seemed so sure of it, too.

But that conviction didn't stop him from swallowing that vial, burning a hole in his larynx, wrecking a kidney or two, failing every final exam, costing Dad a major contract when he had to leave the middle of a software sales pitch to drive down the coast. I, on the other hand, was already in San Francisco, in Hideki's grad student apartment. He wanted it that way. He intended me to be the first art critic on the scene of his final masterpiece.

I just found him sooner than he intended. Rough luck for him.

Standing in the shrine, I can't get the image of Hideki lying in the hospital bed, a tube down his throat, out of my mind. His arrow-slitted eyes. His hand squeezing my wrist, fingers lining up on the old familiar bruises from him—one, two, three, four, five—like he had done when we were children, his eyes burning with hatred, his mouth smirking as he told me I'd always be the unwanted shadow in his sunlight. Except this time, he was the one who was fading fast.

The memory is uncontrollable here, in this unfamiliar place. But maybe there's something to what Kenji said about his practice—about giving his troubles over to something outside himself. I don't believe in gods and spirits, despite the hours I've spent at Saint Isaac's mandatory daily chapel time. But I'm tired of walking around with these memories in me, throbbing like a knife I never bothered to pull from my back.

I'm just so tired. Of not being able to eat or sleep or to chase all these thoughts from my head. Tired of not finding the right trigger to pull to get the revenge that I'm due.

A sign spells out in English how, exactly, to go about honoring the *kami* in the shrine. I start by scooping water into a ladle from a nearby trough, and pour it over my right hand, then my left, then pour water into my cupped hand to use to swish out my mouth. The chilly water raises gooseflesh along my arms, and I nearly drop the slippery ladle as I try to replace it in the trough. The priest's back is to me, but I swear I can see his shoulders tense at my clumsiness.

Next up: the shrine itself. I step up to the outer edge of the shrine and peer through the wooden doorway to the inner sanctum. I'm not allowed inside—instead, I'm supposed to drop some coins in the offering box, bow twice, clap twice to get the *kami*'s attention, pray, and bow one more time. When I reach the prayer part, I stutter for a moment. Am I supposed to address Emperor Meiji? Some other spirit or deity? The universe at large?

Dear world. I feel weird holding my hands clasped in front of me, so I hook one finger in a loose belt loop on my jeans. The hatred burns like napalm in my chest. *Help me find a way to get my revenge*, I pray.

I don't know what I expected. To feel like a stone slab had been lifted off my chest, maybe, or for the perpetual antidepressants fog in my head to clear? But nothing like that happens. Nothing happens at all. What a silly waste.

I turn and walk away without bowing again. Tears prickle in the corners of my eyes. So stupid. I briefly allowed myself to hope. There is no hope for me. I must seek out my revenge on the world alone.

But I don't know if I have the courage. I don't know if I can see it through. I am nothingness. An empty vessel. The core of me is rotted away, and I can never get it back. There's nothing left to fill me but anger. There's nothing left for me to sense but pain.

Another breeze lifts the stray tendrils of hair away from

my face and neck, and a cold wind reaches inside the gaps of my clothes. I raise my head, looking around the square. The prayer boards sway and clatter; the tree leaves beyond the shrine's square shush against each other in a fervent roar. My heart is beating like a drum inside of me—a dark rhythm, goading me on. My blood is on fire; my mind is buzzing as if my dark thoughts were wasps, circling, circling—

And then they collide inside me, like a thunderclap.

I stagger forward. For a moment it feels like I'm falling out of my body, like I might just keep falling. But then the buzzing and drumming subsides, and I find my balance. The priest—he's shouting at me. He props his rake against a sign and charges toward me, his wide, pleated skirt giving the impression that he's floating. He's saying something—I imagine it's some variation of *hey, you*—but the only thing clear is that he's gravely upset.

"*Sumimasen,*" I say, over and over. *I'm sorry. Excuse me.* "*Wakari masen.*" *I don't understand.*

"He's asking if you're okay. He says that you looked like you were about to faint," Kenji says, stepping through the outer gates. His sketchbook's tucked under one arm and his backpack is slung on the opposite shoulder.

"What the fuck, Kenji." I turn from the priest to him. "Are you stalking me?"

Kenji says something to the priest in soft, even tones.

Amerika-jin juts out, an ugly boulder in the otherwise even stream of Japanese. *American.*

Whatever Kenji says next, though, softens him. Kenji bows at the waist to him. *"Dōmo sumimasen-desuita."*

I stare at Kenji, one eyebrow cocked.

"He's trying to teach you about the double—no. Mm. The *dual* nature of the *kami.* He wants you to understand that every *kami*—every spirit—has two natures, all right? That when you respect them, then they are more than happy to love and nurture and care for you. But he is worried you have a—mm, how did he phrase it? A darkened neglect in your heart."

Darkened neglect in my heart? I laugh like dry leaves rattling. Yeah, he's really got my number there. "Whatever. It's not like I believe in that shit."

Kenji makes a strained expression. "It doesn't matter what you believe in, Reiko. If you feel angry, if you're destructive, then you draw anger and destruction to you. Your mindset creates your reality, no matter what you believe."

I gust out my breath, blowing stray hairs out of my face. "Well, then that's just fantastic. Really great. I was just trying to—fuck it. Never mind." I shove past Kenji and head out the outer gates of the square, but he stays right at my side. "You said it always made you feel better to give your problems over to them."

"To let *go* of my problems," Kenji says. "It is the act of releasing them. Not dumping them all over someone else."

"Fine. Whatever. Quit following me everywhere, okay? I don't need you making excuses for me. And it's creepy."

Kenji hesitates, tugging at the strap of his backpack. "I, ahh, I have to follow you."

I stop walking. "Excuse me?"

Kenji lowers his head, a dark fringe of hair concealing his eyes. "Satori-san. He said we aren't ever allowed to let you go anywhere by yourself, because of . . . ahh, because of your condition, and he . . ."

"Oh my God. Are you kidding me? He told you all that?" The chill from the breeze is gone; instead, I'm burning up, from the inside out. The smoldering coals of my hatred are crackling to life again, shifting and sparking with fresh fury.

Kenji doesn't answer. He won't meet my eyes. Just another coward, same as me. Why don't they beat him down, too? Why does he still give a damn?

"I figured out your superhero's secret power," I tell him. My power. My anger, burning me up. I'm going to make as much of a mess as possible when I leave—smear them all with a stain they can't scrub out. "She destroys everything she touches. And everyone."

I will master Hideki's path of vengeance. I will make everyone listen to the dark pounding of my heart.

CHAPTER THREE

THERE ARE SO MANY WAYS TO KILL MYSELF IN Japan—ways to make it matter, make it sting. Suicide isn't a bad way to make my point, as long as I make others suffer for it. I could find it at the end of a cord—an electric kettle's cord, perhaps, because Aunt and Uncle Satori won't let me near anything longer. I picture myself crumpled in the alleyway beneath their ninth-floor apartment in Shinjuku, though it turns out, all the windows are painted shut. Plus, I'd never see Chloe's face when she hears what became of me. I'd never get to nestle in that dark guilt that would forever weight her steps.

But if I did it—if I killed myself—then I'd really have myself a coup. I'd be the first Azumi child to succeed at something.

Hideki tried and failed. Anyway, I want my death to hurt far more than just me. I'm hoping that in Kuramagi, I can find just the right way.

This trip will be good for you girls, Uncle Satori told us while he helped us pack. *Maybe you can learn to get along.* Like we're two puzzle pieces he can force together, and not vinegar and blood. We meet up with Mariko, Kenji, and Kazuo at the main Tokyo *shinkansen* station and wait for the rip of air as the bullet train arrives. (Tadashi is too good to travel by such plebian means; he's going to drive his Range Rover down later in the day.) Mariko pops into the convenience shop and returns with a plastic bag full of triangular *onigiri* and starts nibbling on one while we wait for our train. Kazuo and Aki stand too close to each other while they watch videos on Kazuo's phone. Kenji reads a thick manga compilation. And I wonder what it would be like to be struck by a *shinkansen* train while it's whirring along at 200 miles an hour.

The train hisses into the station. Disgorges its passengers. The cleaners walk down the aisles, collecting any trash left behind and washing down headrests. The seats lift up and swivel around to face the opposite way. Sterile, sleek, empty. Everything moving in flawless concert. Perfection through repetition. I press the bruises on my wrist. One, two, three, four, five.

The train ride is a blur of scenery and noise—Chloe's playlist again, double-bass drumming its way to the speed of our train. Mariko punches away at the cell phone novel she's always working on—short dribs and drabs of words pushed out to her subscribers, chronicling the ups and downs of a water hostess in Tokyo. She tried explaining the plot to me, but it sounded more melodramatic than my old Legends of Eldritch Journey role-playing forums, which is really saying something.

I am flinging across the length of the island of Honshu as my thoughts churn ever inward on themselves, ever fixed on single points.

You've made a mistake, Chloe's email had said, that day it all went to hell. *Everyone needs to see you for what you really are.*

Not who. What. And what they needed to see, apparently, was the monster who'd been lurking in their midst all along.

The email came the week before winter break. Two months after Chloe and her new girlfriend, Selena, shredded up my heart with their pyramid-studded belts. Two months after I left those shreds in Portland, amidst the rainwater flecked with blood and broken glass. Not three days after my early decisions arrived from Stanford and RISD—a yes and a wait list, not that I cared about college. I wanted to go there to develop my art, but none of that mattered anymore. Chloe had pulled my art out of my soul as if it were a thread she'd unraveled herself. Was it even mine, or only something I'd done because she put the brush in my hand? If it had been up to me, would I have made it at all?

When I saw the paintings I made at summer camp with Chloe again, that week before winter break, all I felt was shame. They weren't for the student body of Saint Isaac's to see. What were they doing plastered all over the school? The rotten thing inside of me had gotten loose. Someone had smeared it across Saint Isaac's halls. Why was everyone pointing, cupping hands around their mouths as their eyes followed me? How did they know they were mine? Why weren't they looking at the teachers, hurrying to pull the paintings down? It wasn't until I reached homeroom that I saw Chloe's message on my phone.

Then the security guards came for me.

"We've received some unsettling information about you, Miss Azumi," the principal said. Deacon Karlsson, a man as gaunt and Scandinavian as his name, sat across the desk from me, pretending the conversation was strictly between the two of us and didn't include the three nuns and four security guards crammed into the back of the room. "Some credible information that you mean to do your fellow students harm."

I was too stunned to respond. I'd never before considered doing anything like the collages and paintings portrayed. Those were private works—things created in the dead of night in the studio spaces of camp. I hadn't even turned them in as part of my final portfolio. They were a wonderful secret, a bond between only Chloe and me.

"Your painting with photographs of the senior class says,

and I'm quoting here, 'Everyone must pay for their crimes,'"
Deacon Karlsson said.

Oh, God. I felt the floor opening up beneath me, the lurch before the roller coaster rushed down.

"I'm sure you understand why I've had to contact your parents. And the police."

The world turned into a metallic buzz around me. I couldn't breathe or feel or see. Just noise, crackling like a downed wire in my head. So much noise.

It was better that way.

❖

The train glides to a stop, and we board a smaller local train. A stop in a pristine bathroom at a train station, the toilet playing pop music at me while I pee. A bus. All the while, Mariko, Kazuo, Aki, and Kenji chattering. I chug another Suntory Boss, the only thing I think I might be able to keep down, while Mariko works her way through several more *onigiri*.

WELCOME TO THE KURAMAGI RYOKAN!

We stand in the front entrance of the traditional bed and breakfast, a *ryokan*, that Tadashi had booked for us at the sort of nightly rates so high I had trouble translating them into dollars. ("Some Sony execs love to host retreats at this place," he'd said. "Lots of opportunity here.") The girl at the front counter isn't at all what I'd expected: American, dark-skinned, naturally tightly curled hair cropped close to her head, smiling, confident. Gorgeous. Speaking English. I kick off my shoes with the rest of our crew, tuck them in a cubby, and slip on plastic red slippers.

"My name's Sierra. You marked 'English' on your language preference card, but I'm happy to speak with you in Japanese if you prefer." She glances down at the card in front of her. "Is Mr. Itoyama here?"

"He'll be arriving later." Aki slides across the gleaming wooden floors to the clerk's counter. "I can check us in." They switch into Japanese, and Sierra follows along flawlessly, her intonation sounding—to my ears, at least—as good as any I've heard. Suddenly Sierra stands up from the desk and starts up a narrow staircase, everyone following her closely. I scramble to keep up.

"Can you explain in English, too?" I ask, even as a hot shame washes over me. "Please?"

She flashes a smile at me. "Sure. I'm just showing you all to your rooms."

We reach the top of the staircase. It looks over the front gardens of the *ryokan*, running along the main street of Kuramagi village. "Kuramagi was once a thriving village along the old postal route between Kyoto and Tokyo during the shogunate period," Sierra says, then repeats herself in Japanese.

"Kuramagi was one of the first villages to choose to preserve its historic appearance by not permitting any electric lights outdoors and burying all cables. The village works hard to retain its original Edo-period feel."

I look out the opened windows at the multi-tiered garden beneath us: small stone statues, koi ponds, bristly bushes turning autumn shades. The main street of the town is lined in dark and white wood buildings, few of them more than two or three stories tall, with narrow vertical strips of wood across most windows and steep roofs of overlapping tiles ending in fancy, swirling caps.

"At night, we ask that you please be indoors no later than ten. The village is lit with gas lamps at that time, and it's very dark, so for your protection, it's safer to remain indoors. We will lock the doors to the *ryokan* each night at ten."

Sierra turns to the row of sliding thin wood and rice paper panels set back from the windows and twists a small piece of metal in the center of one panel's edge. "Ladies, this will be your room. I'll give you a moment to drop off your things. Then please come meet me downstairs. Gentlemen, come with me, please." Sierra and the boys disappear back down the stairs.

The panel slides open to reveal a traditional sitting room: rice paper–paneled walls, tatami mats on the floor, and three pallets like the one I sleep on at the Satoris' apartment lined up against one wall. Akiko immediately heads toward the one closest to the window. "I'll take this one." She picks one of the casual robes, a *yukata*, off the stack and tosses it at me.

"I can't believe we have to be inside by ten," Mariko says. "This is going to be so lame."

Akiko rolls her eyes. "We're not following that." She punches at her phone. "Tadashi says there's a great club the next village over. A real one, not a sad thing like when we went to Nagano."

"But Sierra said they lock the *ryokan* doors at ten," I say.

"Yeah. The doors." Akiko slides open the window. "You'll stay here and let us in, won't you, Rei-Rei?"

I glimpse a wonderful fantasy. A dark, hateful world— monsters pursuing Aki through the streets of Kuramagi. She's trapped in the darkened garden, thick, sinuous shadows coiling around her. *Please, let me in!* she screams, while the shadows carve deep furrows into her flesh. *Reiko, help!*

If only. I smile, imagining my teeth thick and bright as a shark's. "Of course I will."

The screams echo in my thoughts while I unpack. The path of hatred carves deeper, greased on thoughts of Aki's pain.

"So what are you planning to do around here?" Sierra asks, while I sit in the lobby and wait on Aki and Mariko to finish priming for dinner and their inevitable nightclub trip later tonight.

I close the magazine I'd been flipping through. "Do?" I laugh, throaty. "Follow my cousin around, I guess. She's the exciting one."

"Sorry, you came to the wrong town if you're looking for excitement. People come here to relax."

"Fine." I smile in spite of myself. She's easy to talk to, and not just for her English. Again I feel that tug in my gut, pulling at the space where my attraction to human beings used to be. But the antidepressants have hollowed me out. "What relaxing things are there to do around here?"

"Well, there are the *onsen*s, of course. Natural hot springs along the mountainside. Mister Onagi owns a couple of them, and he'll rent them out to you guys by the hour. There's the hiking trail that runs between this town and the next one on the old postal route . . ." She drums her mint-green nails on the counter. "You can always check out the historical museum. It's in the old travelers' inn down the road. Or there's the *shinju* shrine, if you're feeling morbid."

Like I'm ever not. "What do you mean?"

"Oh—I figured you knew about it. It's why a lot of people come to Kuramagi, aside from the festival. It's a monument to two doomed lovers, you know, a Romeo and Juliet thing." Sierra's eyes roll. "They, like, pray to the doomed lovers to bless their own relationships. Pretty twisted, if you ask me, but it keeps me employed, right?"

I curl back, my mouth suddenly parched. "Oh." I force myself to swallow. "Is that why you live here?"

"Please, are you kidding? I don't live here. Just work here a couple afternoons a week." Sierra smiles again. "I teach English a few towns from here. No, I think you have to be a special brand of disturbed to live in Kuramagi."

"Because of the shrine?" I ask.

"Sure, that's part of it. But mostly they're such sticklers about the whole historical setting. And then there's the curfew . . ." Sierra closes her hand on the counter into a fist, and leans forward, checking the hallway toward the dining rooms. "Like, don't tell Mr. Onagi I said so, but they get so caught up in preserving history around here that I think they sometimes forget the rest of the world's moved on."

I nod and fiddle with the belt on my *yukata*. Stuck in time, unable to move forward. I know the feeling well. My thoughts are buzzing, wordless, in the back of my mind.

"It's just creepy, is all. Stick around here a couple days—I bet you'll see what I mean." She looks toward the staircase that leads toward our room, her extra-wide smile returning. "Welcome back, ladies! Are you ready for me to show you to your dining room?"

Aki and Mariko clomp downstairs. Even though they're wearing their *yukata*, they're clearly wearing another outfit underneath, and Aki's makeup is thick as ever. Mariko's three-inch platforms jut out of her handbag.

Sierra leads us to the dining room, reminds us to take off our slippers, and explains a few of the dishes. Our dining room is traditional-style as well, with small legless chairs propped around a low table. I survey the explosion of tiny ceramic plates before me. Pickled radish, maybe? That one definitely holds sashimi, though I'm not sure what type of fish it is. Raw beef, which may or may not end up cooked before the night is out. All the sorts of food I'd have loved to devour, before I lost my taste for everything.

And—raisins?

"Those are really good," Aki says, leaning over my shoulder. "Miniature sugar dates."

But when I pick them up, I see the tiny legs on their undersides.

I narrow my eyes at Akiko and pop them in my mouth. Grin darkly as her upper lip curls back.

"Eww, I can't believe you ate them!" Aki squeals, as I finish off the bowl. "Don't you know what those were? They were wasp larvae. Wasps."

As I stare Aki down, I imagine I can feel the wasps buzzing inside me, angry, churning with an acute need to strike. A fitting image. I'm starting to feel in control of my hate again. "I know now," I say.

Mr. Onagi's workers bring out our next courses. Beautiful,

fresh fish; vegetables carved like blossoms. I want to enjoy it, but I know it'll taste the same as everything else these days—ashy and dead, sucking the saliva right out of my mouth. Everything sticks in my throat like a too-large pill.

"We'll go to the lovers' shrine tomorrow," Aki says. "It's supposed to be a beautiful place for photographs. Very scenic."

Translation: if the photographs don't serve her purpose, it'll be my fault. I may not have learned Japanese yet, but I'm getting fluent in Akiko.

I clench a pale sliver of raw fish, translucent and shimmering like a shell, between my chopsticks. I have to eat. Everyone else is scarfing down rice and *shabu-shabu* slices of beef, roasted trout, pickled plums and ginger and radishes. I want to eat it all, but I'm so full, I've gorged on my anger and hatred, I feel like I'm vibrating out of my skin. I've shoved my anger down for so long and there aren't any pockets of my body left for me to tuck it away—

The lights flicker overhead. Mariko squeaks; everyone glances up, food dangling from their chopsticks and broth spilling from their spoons.

The buzzing in the back of my head intensifies.

Maybe my anger is making me hallucinate, but somehow, I can't shake the feeling that I made the lights flicker.

Embrace it, a voice whispers from within me, Chloe's voice, and I let the buzzing take me over. I am the earthquake. I am destruction. The buzzing in my head grows.

"Worthless old building," Kazuo says. "This whole village is lame. What's the big deal with preserving it anyway? Who cares about the past?"

Something rumbles behind us, like a truck shoving its way down the narrow street. No—now it's rumbling *into* the wooden *ryokan* building. It's rolling up through the floor and rattling our plates and sending the pendant lamp bouncing furiously. Mariko scrambles into Kazuo's lap. The glass bottle of sake crashes off of the table's edge and shatters. One shard of glass strikes Akiko on the wrist, and she screams.

I sink back into my chair and pretend I called the earthquake to swallow me up. How wonderful it feels to imagine my body tearing apart, wrenched open by the ground itself.

But within seconds, it's over. Everyone's frozen, waiting for more. When nothing else happens, they all start talking at once, frantic in Japanese. Through the thin walls, we can hear chatter in the other dining rooms as well. Kenji rushes over to Akiko with a damp napkin and twists it around her wrist, then helps her to her feet.

"Hello? Is everyone all right?" Mr. Onagi is knocking on the door to our dining room. "Anyone hurt?"

Akiko screeches a reply in Japanese. Tadashi finally stands and rushes to Akiko's other side, and he and Kenji carry her from the dining room like they're rescuing her from a burning building.

I help myself to another scoop of rice, savoring the buzz in my head and the rattle in my bones. The egg of my anger has cracked open, runny yolk spilling out, and suddenly I feel better than I've felt in weeks. I take a bite of food. I was meant to come to Kuramagi after all. Maybe, just maybe, it can give me the strength—fill me with enough hatred—to do what I have to do.

I'll make them all sorry. I'll find a way to make them pay for their cruelty, their neglect. I'll make sure they never forget me or what I've done.

CHAPTER FOUR

SOMETHING IS HITTING THE THIN WINDOW OF OUR *ryokan* room, tapping like a skeletal branch. I blink, groggy, still feeling pinned in place by the thick vines of my dreams—dreams of lava and steam, of the valley filling with blood as the earth rumbles and I raise my hands up high. But it's all gone now. Everything is dark and a deeper dark, all swirling together, until finally I spot the square of weak dishwater-gray moonlight coming from the window.

Plink. Plink.

I throw off the heavy duvet and force myself to my feet, though my muscles feel shot through with lead. My head is still buzzing, more insistent than ever in the room's cavernous silence. I stagger toward the window. *Plink.* I jerk back, startled, as a pebble hits the window again.

Mariko and Aki. Of course. I glance over my shoulder; their pallets are still empty. It takes me a few seconds to figure out the window latch, then I slide it open and narrowly dodge another pebble aimed right for my head.

"Took you long enough!" Aki hisses up at me from the ground floor garden. A sheet of fog is tucked tight against the ground, so the girls look legless, floating toward me from the lamp-lit ancient world of Kuramagi. The air tastes heavy with impending rain. I know the souvenir shop is just on the other side of the narrow street from us, but all I can see is the dull halo of its lantern now, the darkness and fog is so thick.

Mariko hoists Aki up onto her shoulders, then Aki rolls onto the roof of the first-floor porch. I catch her by her bandaged hand, and contemplate letting go.

It'd serve her right, but I yank her through the window. That's not how I want to get my revenge.

The lantern at the souvenir shop quavers; a deeper shadow cuts through the fog, stirring up the smooth butter-spread calm along the road. *Let it in*, something says from inside of me. Just like the earthquake.

I frown and lean back from the window. Am I seeing things again? Hearing them? A bitter voice answers me inside my head. *Idiot. Of course you are. Just like you think you can cause lights to flicker. Like you can summon earthquakes with your hate.* It's not Chloe's voice this time but Hideki's, which never fails to remind me of how worthless I am. The fog has settled once more, except where Mariko bounces, trying to scramble onto the lower roof. I jut my torso out the window again and help her in.

"You should've gone with us, Rei! The club was so cool! They played great music, and Aki convinced these guys to buy us free drinks because they felt bad about her hand." Mariko shimmies out of her coat. "She should work at a hostess club. She'd make so much money in tips—"

"I'm not working at a hostess club. I'm a star." Even in the dark, I can see the knife glint of Aki's narrowed stare.

Something rustles in the far corner of the room. I can see it outlined in moonlight against the tatami flooring—the sleek black husk of a Japanese roach. Japanese roaches have shells that look thick as a beetle's, and I've seen ones in the Satoris' apartment almost the size of my fist. If we were back there, I'd already be reaching for the spray bottle with a label that is a mystery to me save for the massive exclamation mark at the end and the depiction of what looks like a drunken cartoon roach.

I ignore the roach and give the garden one last look, but the shadows I'd seen have evaporated; the fog is thick and solid. No disturbances, no movement. I latch the window shut again.

"This place is so boring. Even the earthquake was a letdown,"

Aki says. "Only a three, they said at the club. No serious damage."

"Yeah. A real letdown," I say. "Too bad we aren't all dead."

"It's not boring." Mariko exchanges a look with Aki. "It's creepy. That fog . . . it isn't right." The look Aki gives her could pop a zit, but Mariko doesn't back down. They regard each other for a long moment. Then Mariko says, softer, "I'm not just making it up. I'm telling you, I saw—"

"You watch too much anime," Aki says.

Discussion over. I wriggle back into my pallet, and let sleep drag me under again, swaddling me in the thickness of the buzzing inside my head.

I wake up again just after six, slip out of our room, and shuffle toward the communal bathroom in my plastic red slippers to empty my bladder. On my way back out of the restrooms, I run into Mr. Onagi as he unlocks the front door to the *ryokan*. "I trust you slept well after last night's earthquake?" he asks me in English.

I nod.

"I'm very glad. Some people your age find our curfew boring. But it's for the best for everyone."

God. Everyone acts like roving bands of vagrants sweep through the town at night, emboldened by the lack of streetlights. "What do you mean, it's for the best?"

His leathery face scrunches up. "Well, it's how we keep the village safe." Then he smoothes his expression. "But no matter.

You are here for the cultural festival, yes? I expect a lot more guests will arrive tonight."

"Yeah. Can't wait." I grimace and shove my hands into my pockets. "Actually, I thought I might go for a walk," I say.

"Sure, sure. I'll have breakfast ready in an hour. If you like, though, you should visit the historical museum. They open at seven." He jabs a thumb to the right down the main road. "Might want to get your walking done early. It's supposed to rain."

Poor Aki and her photo shoot plans. I head upstairs to dress, then come back down and sit on the porch steps to lace up my boots, before I head into the narrow streets.

The fog is gone, though woolly thunderheads sheathe the mountain peaks that pin us in on either side. If I stand perfectly still, I can hear the distant rustle of the river at the valley's base. As I walk through town, I look over my shoulder after every couple of buildings I pass, just to make sure Kenji—or anyone else—isn't following me; now that I know about Uncle Satori's decree, I feel honor-bound to keep them from succeeding.

The village's streets are stacked one atop the other like rice paddies, a stair step of dark tile and wood down the mountainside. I climb a narrow, crooked staircase to reach the next tier up and catch my breath at the fiery burst of fall leaves along the opposite mountain's slope. It really is beautiful here—there's a dull thump inside of me, that feeling that once compelled me to grab my camera and frame up a thousand shots in hopes that just one might capture the awe that I feel. I wish I could feel that again—like I did at night in the studio at camp with Chloe cheering me on. But I think the weight of my hatred has shattered it. I can never feel that again.

The buzzing in my head crowds around my thoughts, a tremor like too much caffeine. I pinch my nose to try to clear it out.

An old woman, humped back jutting through her parka, makes her way down the steps of a Shinto shrine embedded in a gap between buildings. Zigzag paper lightning bolts dangle over the entrance to the shrine, twisting back and forth as a fresh breeze kicks up and whips my loose hair into my face. The woman glances at me, frowns, then begins her slow crawl down the other side of the street.

The village is more extensive than I first expected. There's a water wheel alongside the mountain stream at one edge of town; countless tiny shops and cafés, their proprietors just now unlatching the window covers and setting out their signs. Their persistence in keeping the historical feel to the town has been successful. If it weren't for the occasional Toyota crawling along the road, I'd feel lost in time.

Finally I pass a sign for the KURAGAMI HISTORICAL HONJIN AND HERITAGE MUSEUM. It's set back from the road behind a gateway that opens onto a spare garden. A gray-haired woman is polishing the dark wooden doors, but stops and bows to me with an *"Ohayō-gozai-masu." Good morning.*

"*Ohayō-gozai-masu,*" I reply, then decide to press my luck, "*Hakubutsukan, aite-masu-ka?*" *Is the museum open?*

She tilts her head, momentarily flustered, then answers me in a steady stream of Japanese until I hold up my hand.

"*Sumimasen desuka eigo de hanasemasu-ka?*" *Can you speak English?*

That flicker of surprise. "Please, come inside. I am just now starting the fire."

I follow her indoors. The main chamber of the room is two stories tall, its tatami mat floor raised on a platform, with a massive chain dangling down from the roof and holding a cauldron. She prods the cauldron's contents with a poker, inviting a gust of smoke into the room. "This *honjin* was built in 1804 to host imperial and shogunate guests who passed through Kuramagi," she says. "This is the main room of the traveler's inn, where the travelers and the family who lived here would gather. Seating depended on a person's rank. They would sit farthest from the direction of the smoke if they were very important, or in the smoke's path if they were of low ranking."

I laugh in spite of myself. Nothing like a case of black lung to keep those filthy peasants in line.

"The women of this inn have wiped down the walls every day since it was built in order to clean off the smoke, like this." She demonstrates with her rag, running it along the gleaming wood. Sure enough, I can see a line out of arm's reach where the dark wood changes from perfectly polished to smoky and charred, though it's just barely visible on the near-black wood. "Do you know why we have the wooden slats on the windows?" she asks me.

I shake my head.

"They are specially angled. The inhabitants inside the building can see out, but a person on the street cannot see in. In the shogun times, this was very useful!"

I grin again. "Why? What did they have to hide?"

"Some people in the town supported the emperor. They did not want the shogunate to rule any longer. So it was good to know if anyone was coming who might hear them plotting against the *bakufu*—the military government that supported the shogun."

History has never been my forté, but Japanese history, even less so. We never got much in school in America beyond what happened in World War II. And Mom and Dad would sooner get a colonoscopy than talk about their lives before they came to college in the States. I run my finger along the length of one of the slats. "Oh. I guess I thought you meant because of . . . like, swords and arrows and stuff." As soon as I say it, I wish I could stuff the words back in my mouth. A dumb American tourist, she can probably forgive. But a dumb Japanese-American one? Inexcusable.

"No, no. Life was peaceful here under the shogunate. Peaceful, but . . ." She lets the rag dangle limp in her hands.

"Stagnant. The *bakufu*'s warrior class, the samurai, were bored without battles to fight. They caused problems sometimes for people trying to make their lives better." Her expression darkens. "And a bored samurai, especially one part of the Tokugawa shogunate, could be a very dangerous thing indeed."

My grip tightens around the slats. I remember the way Hideki looked on his first home leave from Iraq, before he got his early discharge. A medic without a body to mend. A weapon without anyone to fire it. Once again I can feel the five points on my arm striking a dissonant chord. A fighter will always find himself a new fight.

"The Tokugawa shogunate ruled everything. The emperor was only a puppet on their strings. We were a military country then, but some people—like the residents of this house—fought to restore the emperor's right to rule."

"And why did people want the emperor to be in power again?" I ask, trying to keep my tone light.

"The emperor wanted to befriend the West and make Japan a superpower. Not a lonely island. After your American Admiral Perry arrived with his *kurofune*—the black ships—and tried to force Japan to open itself to trade, the shogunate wanted to close off even further. But the emperor's supporters wanted to join the rest of the world and gain even more power for Japan."

I laugh. Well, I guess I know who won. Emperor Meiji and his grand Restoration and his shrine in Yoyogi Park.

"If you go upstairs, you can see the secret panel," she says, bunching up her rag once more. "It's blocked now, but it leads to the attic room where the emperor's supporters would gather and plan to overthrow the shogunate."

I thank her for the tour and make my way back downstairs. Part of me is itching to have a camera in my hand once more so I can document the weak sunlight filtering through the open rooms, the details carved into the wooden beams overhead, the paintings and scrolls. But I'm done with that life. I lace my boots back up and head onto the streets.

I collide with Kenji on my way back down to the *ryokan*'s street level, nearly knocking us both down the narrow stairs. "Rei!" he cries. "Where the hell have you been? I've been looking for you everywhere! You wouldn't answer your phone, and you didn't say anything to Aki and Mariko—"

"You didn't call Uncle Satori, did you?" I make fists inside my hoodie pockets. The last thing I need is him thinking his impromptu "suicide watch" needs to be doubled up.

Kenji hesitates, Adam's apple quivering against the collar of his shirt. He smells of warmth and soap; I notice his damp hair slick against his head, and realize he's just come from the shower. His shirt clings to him in damp patches, revealing more muscle beneath than I would've guessed.

"No," he finally says. "And I won't. Not unless you force

me to." He looks me square in the eye. "Don't force me to, okay?"

Don't give him a reason to think I'm sneaking off to hurt myself, he means. Because my parents and Uncle Satori conscripted him to spy on me. I shrug and look away.

"Reiko."

I look up at those deep brown eyes, the fine planes of his nose. I try not to see him as another jailor, another thing for me to hate. But it's hard. I can't pull away the red filter that warps every memory I make.

"I've seen what you can do with a camera. The collages you used to make."

Shame billows inside of me. "How did you see those—"

"The ones of Seattle. You know? The black-and-white photos that you painted on and stitched together. I thought it was really cool."

Oh—he means the ones from before art camp, before Chloe and the collages that landed me in the psychiatric ward. I forgot those were still online, on that cheesy little ArtSpace site I'd created to serve as my portfolio for RISD. The ones that were only good enough to get me wait-listed.

"If you have a gift like that, you should use it," Kenji says. "Pay the bills with Aki's stuff and Satori-san's work, sure, but you could do so much more. It must be incredible, to see the world the way you see it."

"You mean the way I *saw* the world." I smile, sticky as

honey. "But that world's gone, so why worry about capturing it? Let's give Aki what she wants."

❖

"Give me the map. Just give me the goddamned map," Aki snarls, and follows it up with a flurry of Japanese words that I'm quite certain I've never heard before. "We have to do the photos at the lovers' shrine. It's so tragic and romantic."

Tadashi surrenders the map to her. We've been wandering the forests beneath the lowest tier of Kuramagi for half an hour now, trying to find the lovers' shrine before the black woolly clouds overhead split open and soak Aki and her rented silk kimono. I squint down at my English version of the hiking map, which helpfully marks such features as "Moon Waterfall" and "Teahouse" farther down the trail, but doesn't list the alleged lovers' shrine at all. The only thing close to the *ryokan* and the village proper is the untranslated *Shinjū-hokora*. It depicts two green fingers of stone yoked together with rope, which seems vaguely like it could depict lovers. All the same, I can't figure out how we reach it from the trail we're on, or if it even connects at all.

"This way," Tadashi says. "Hurry up."

We trudge behind him down the same slope we climbed two minutes before.

The slender branchless cedar trunks cause some sort of eerie optical illusion in my peripheral vision as they slide past. Wet, moldy scents soak the air around us; the too-ripe stink of early autumn surrounds us with rot and decay. That, coupled with the buzzing in my head, now a raging hornet's nest, keeps me perpetually on the cliff of feeling like I might throw up. I never ate breakfast after I visited the museum so I could get the women's bathing room to myself. I want to eat comfortably, like I did last night, but now the thought of making myself eat feels awful again. My hunger is turning ragged in my gut, slicing me up from the inside.

I trip over a loose stone on the trail; when I glance down, I notice a crooked line fracturing the stone path, probably split open by the earthquake. Sure enough, as I look through the trees farther up the slope, a narrow furrow runs through the undergrowth, then halts at a sagging, moss-strewn boulder. The boulder looks as if the earthquake pried it forward; feathery torn vines fringe its edges. It looks so inviting, like the perfect place to curl up and hide from the world for a while. I lean toward it.

The buzz in my head rises in cadence.

"Are you guys sure this is the way?" Mariko says. "My feet hurt. Maybe we should do this another day . . ."

Her voice tapers off in the distance as I step off the path, onto the mountain's slope. I want to see what's behind the boulder. All I can hear is the crunch of leaves under my feet like snapping bones. Everything smells loamy and close to death, like fruit just about to ferment. It smells wonderful. It smells the way I feel inside.

I run my hand along the boulder. An involuntary shudder wracks through me, though there's no breeze, no chill. There's a hollow space tucked behind it, just like I'd hoped. Stone and dirt, ripe with a metallic tang. The buzzing has turned to a chorus now, a pressure guiding me in.

Someone's calling my name, but it's too quiet. All I hear is my own heartbeat, throbbing in my ears. All I feel is the pressure in my head, threatening to pop.

I step into the hollow just as the sky opens up and the rain thunders against the forest canopy.

It looks like some sort of shrine inside the hollow—at least, to my untrained eyes. Only a weak, watery light grazes against the paving stones crusted with dirt and the carved altar pressed against the far wall. But none of the other items I've grown to associate with Shinto shrines are present—none of the zigzag streamers, the prayer boards, the offering boxes, or recessed spaces for the *kami* to rest. Just that altar, splattered with dried moss and vines and roots that curl down from the hollow's roof.

Then I spot a stone: black speckled with gray, round on one end, curved, shaped like a comma. The buzzing in my head mingles with the sounds of rain. Something inside me shifts—a weary sigh, a head falling against a pillow after an exhausting day.

I reach for it easily, my body a resounding chorus of *yes*.

❖

Someone is calling my name again. I push myself up from the altar—when had I knelt before it?—and turn toward the opening into the makeshift *hokora*, the tiny Shinto shrine. My sandals skitter across the stones as I peer down the slope toward the postal trail.

"Hurry up! You need to get inside!"

"I'm coming!" I shout, unable to keep my annoyance from curling the edges of the syllables. I just want a moment alone—it's all I ever want—but of course there's always more work to be done. I hope Aki's kimono is ruined by the storm, her makeup running clownish trails down her face. I close my fist tight around the stone, duck around the boulder—I fit around it more easily this time—and start down the wooden path to meet them on the trail.

It's not until I stop to lift the skirts of my burgundy *iromuji* that I realize I just answered in Japanese without thinking. And that I'm wearing a burgundy *iromuji*.

And that the woman waiting for me on the trail, her finely patterned kimono immaculate even as rain pelts her, is not Akiko.

CHAPTER FIVE

"YOUR CHORES AROUND THE *HONJIN* ARE STILL NOT finished," she says, shuffling ahead of me in small but furious steps. "And yet you play at that foolish shrine. It's disgraceful. Your father is soft for allowing you to go on this way."

My father. I know, with a conviction I haven't earned, that this woman isn't talking about Tetsuo Azumi. How could she be? I don't know how, but I know it as certainly as I know my own name. Which is—

"Miyu!" the woman hisses again. "You're slower than spring thaw! Hurry up! Do you really want to disappoint him?"

Miyu. No. That isn't right. I'm Reiko—Reiko Azumi, daughter of Tetsuo and Yuki Azumi of suburban Seattle, Washington. But Miyu feels right; like an old nickname, maybe, something a friend had called me once as a joke and then it suited me so well it stuck.

No. What am I thinking? I'm dumbly following some grumpy older woman who is calling me by the wrong name. What about my—my co-workers? (My mind hitches as if over a snagged stitch at the thought of calling them friends.) Akiko and Kenji and Mariko and the rest. I stop and turn, searching for them, but there is no sign. I fumble with the *iromuji* kimono's massive, billowing sleeves as I reach for my throat. My camera is gone. What the hell? Wrong clothes, wrong name—what is going on?

"If you do not come with me right this moment, you will not like what happens," the woman says, with a voice like charcoal. I clatter after her, all too aware of the noise of my wooden sandals—when did I put those on?—against stone and the way I feel I might tip over with every step.

The rain sounds worse than it feels; the high canopy of trees absorbs most of the moisture. Maybe Akiko's kimono will be spared after all. Maybe they've already headed for shelter, too. All right—I'll follow this lady, figure out what has her panties all in a wad (is she wearing panties under her robe? Am I?), then find the others. Simple enough.

Or so it seems, until we reach the trail's mouth and turn onto the main streets of Kuramagi.

Hundreds of people pour through the streets like a spilled bag of grain. Men and women of every age, but every last one of them clad in traditional kimonos—navy and red and green and patterned. This girl wears an elegantly embroidered formal kimono called a *furisode*, for the cultural festival perhaps, and that man has the wide folded skirt of a *hakama*—not that I have the first clue when I'd learned the distinction. Pack horses haul carts of caged chickens or grain or fabric down the streets. Ribbons of smoke spin from every chimney and hut; a sweet starchy smell radiates from one of the shops we pass, enticing me to linger in spite of the rain.

Is this part of the cultural festival? The opening ceremony isn't until tomorrow, but maybe today is some kind of unofficial reenactment or something, chock full of cosplayers. I can't find a single person in jeans or hear the telltale twinkling cell phone sounds, but maybe that's part of the reenactment rules.

And at some point, I must have agreed to participate, too. God. First I think I can cause earthquakes, then I start having blackouts where I don't remember changing into feudal villagers' garb. Probably another undocumented side effect of the antidepressants: *agrees to absurd historical reenactments*, right along with *may cause suicidal thoughts and tendencies*. Gotta love modern medicine.

My sandal catches on the uneven stones of the narrow staircase to the village's upper level. I pitch forward and nearly slam my chin into the step in front of me. "Graceless cow," the woman snarls back at me. Like it is my fault these sandals are impossible. I slip my foot back into the sandal—I am wearing *tabi*, I notice, white cotton socks with a separate slot for my big toe—and hurry up the stairs after her.

"Listen," I call. "I think there's been some kind of mistake. I need to get back to my—uhh, my friends, and—and I appreciate the costume, but I—"

"Friends!" She laughs. "A jester, are you? You have no friends."

Well, that cuts a bit close. "I appreciate that you've all gone to a lot of trouble here, but I really don't think I should have a role in your reenactment or whatever. I just—umm, I really need to go. Sorry."

The woman whirls around to face me and seizes a handful of my robe's collar. Shock more than anything pins me in place. The fine white powder dusting her face cracks as she leans in close; I can smell her breath, heavy with tea and rot.

"You had the perfect opportunity to leave us, didn't you? But you chose not to take it. Live with the choices you've made." Her upper lip twitches; she seems to be searching my face for something. "Or do your father a courtesy and relieve him of your burden for good."

The hairs on the back of my neck rise at that. This lady's role-playing skills put the Legends of Eldritch Journey board members to shame. Okay, I decide. I'll see where this goes. It beats tailing Akiko around. And I've never turned down a chance to be someone other than myself.

She's leading me to the *honjin*, I realize. An unbidden sense of dread coils around my throat like a noose. Though I don't know why I feel it, I recognized this sensation all too well—it's like the long walk to the principal's office that day at Saint Isaac's. It's like the moment I first pushed open Hideki's bathroom door. I can't name what fills me with that dread, but I know it lays inside the *honjin* walls.

The woman and I shed our sandals in the front room of the inn, and I drop into a bow without thinking. *"Chichi-ue,"* I say. *Father*. I don't know what chills me more: the word itself or the fact that I'd said it so readily.

"Stand." A shadow drapes across me. "You have work to do."

I rise and find myself face to face with a man who looks nothing like my dad—Tetsuo Azumi, Chief of Digital Product Sales and Development for UpStart Technologies. And yet . . . I can't shake the flare of shame the sight of that face ignites in me. Round nose, wrinkles folded across his face like a fan, thick black hair speckled with gray . . . it's a particular breed of shame. I felt it the first time I'd been informed that my parents were coming to visit me in the psychiatric ward. The shame of facing my parents for the first time since the glass jar where I'd hidden all my secrets had shattered open.

"You are not supposed to leave this house unescorted, Miyu," he tells me. Me—Miyu.

I grip a handful of my thick cotton robe in one hand.

"Uhh . . . I had . . ." I glance toward the woman beside me, her mouth puckers up like a stubborn spring bud. "Yodo-in was with me."

She closes her eyes with a snort of air.

"And your work was not finished when you left," Father says.

I look toward the platform of the main room—the hanging cauldron in the center, issuing a spray of sparks each time a stray raindrop finds its way through the chimney into the embers. The wooden bucket against the wall with a rag draped over it. The black wooden floors, only partly polished, but mostly fuzzed by a thin veneer of soot.

"I have a very important gathering tonight," he says. "I will not allow you to ruin this, too."

Something in his tone makes me tremble like a string he's twanged. "I'm very sorry. I'll finish it right now." I pad up the stairs onto the tatami mat platform and snatch the rag. The scrap trembles in my hands as I dip it into the soapy water.

What kind of crap role have I been assigned for this stupid reenactment? I think. But at the same moment, as I start wiping the wood, up and down, up and down, my muscles find the rhythm like an old familiar warmth. I know this act. I have cherished this act for the silence and peace it brings me. When I do this, I am safe.

My father (the man playing my father?) and the older woman speak in jagged, splintered tones in the other corner of the main room, but I can hear enough to make out what they are talking about. Perhaps that's their intention. "You should send her away," the woman says, her scowl furrowing her brow and flaking the pale makeup on her face. "Our plan is dangerous enough without the sort of complications she always brings. Everything she touches is destroyed."

I grimace. She *really* knows me well.

"That will be for the *daimyo* to decide," my father replies. "She'll be his problem soon enough."

As I bend down to wet the rag again, I feel something pinch my skin inside a hidden pocket of my robe. It's the stone I took from the altar. Something shifts inside me, like my dream of the earth splitting open, and I smile.

Beyond the narrow slats over the windows, voices gather in the streets, shouting something I can't quite make out. I peer through the wooden slats. A pair of horses—tall, proud steeds, unneutered, muscles firm as clay on their chests—push through the throng of peasants and merchants. The faces of the men atop them are shielded from my view, but I recognize the golden three-leaved sigil on the black banner carried by the man in front.

The *Tokugawa*. The shogunate rulers I learned about at the *honjin* historical museum—the same building where I now stand. According to the woman at the museum, they were the ruling family of the shogunate, the Japanese military that, in essence, ruled over Edo-period Japan.

The standard-bearer pulls his horse to a halt just outside our *honjin* and slides from the saddle. After securing his horse, he moves to the two men behind him. They wear the long sleeves of a traveling *haori* jacket in a solemn deep gray; rather than don the broad hats of the villagers, their silky black topknots stand uncovered, at attention.

A new fear trickles into my veins at the sight of these men. Unlike the dull weight of fear I'd felt toward my father, this one jolts me like lightning. A dangerous fear. The kind of fear I never can resist.

"Who is it?" Father asks, frowning as he moves toward the front windows.

The answer comes to me from a deep well that opens inside me, and sounds just as dark. Somehow, I know the name of these men and feel the fear of them, too.

"Samurai."

Father's eyes widen, whites flashing, before he recovers and stares outside. "Not just samurai." His fingers hook in the *obi* that binds his kimono. *"Hatamoto."*

The meaning of the word bubbles up from the dark well, too. The *hatamoto* are samurai who represent the shogunate in Kyoto directly rather than serving a feudal lord. Military officers, immediately responsible to the *bakufu* government.

"What are they doing here?" Yodo hisses. "We received no word of this. If they know of our—"

"Silence," Father says. "They know nothing. The shogun is just rattling his saber at the *daimyo*, like he so loves to do."

"But they could ruin it all. Too much scrutiny—"

"Go," Father says to her. "Send word to the *daimyo*'s clerk. Don't let them see you."

Yodo-in bows, quick and reflexive, as she moves toward the back of our *honjin* to slip away unseen. I glance toward Father and let the crackle of shame I feel when I look at him embolden me. "And what is it you wish for me to do?" I asked.

His jaw goes stiff as steel as his gaze snaps toward mine. I can hear his old lessons, can hear the rap of the bamboo stick against the garden stones as he forced me to recite the seven virtues that I forever seemed to lack. *Filial piety* was always at the top of the virtues I'd violated.

"What I always wish you to do," he says at last, the ice of his tone glistening with a threat. "Serve."

We line up, facing each other, in the front room of the *honjin* to greet the shogun's samurai. Instinct guides me into place; I kneel and bow my head just like Father does.

The samurai enter. I can only see their shoes at first. "Stand," a voice commands.

I do, and slink back to my bucket. My pulse quickens, hatred filling me like oxygen.

"My most humble respects to you, honorable samurai of the Tokugawa," I hear my father say. "To what do we owe the honor of serving you?"

I draw a deep breath as they talk, trying to break whatever spell has been woven over me. I'm not in feudal Japan. There is no great life-or-death conspiracy to overthrow the shogunate hanging in the balance. This stranger cannot order me into service. Who the hell do I think I'm pretending to be? It's always been second nature for me to piece together elaborate backstories for my elven sorceress and cruel space syndicate baroness. I always feel safest playing someone other than myself, but playing a weak, shame-filled character is not why I came to Kuramagi. It's time for me to quit succumbing to distraction and plot my revenge. No more delays.

I toss the rag back into the wooden bucket and head toward the front of the great room to slide back into my wooden *geta* sandals. "Look, I'm sorry," I say, as the door swings open again. "I've got to get back to my friends. You guys have fun with your—"

The two samurai, their squire, and my "father" stare at me as if I've been speaking . . . well, as if I've been speaking English.

Which I have.

But which I *haven't been*, up until this point.

Once again, the throbbing pressure builds up behind my eyes. God. What the hell medication did I take? If I accidentally doubled up on the Xanax, this just might be a really wicked hallucination—

"She speaks the language of the barbarians," the elder

samurai says. His right hand crosses his body and slides to the handle of his *katana*. "Do you allow her to consort with the animals aboard the *kurofune*?"

The American naval vessels, right. Okay, fine, so they're going to scold me for going out of character. I can play along just long enough to find a graceful exit.

"Please forgive my daughter, Goemon-sama," Father says to the older samurai. "She is of a dark disposition, and her sense of humor is lacking." Father's lip curls back so hard I can almost hear it. "Miyu, bring our guests some tea."

"*Hai*, Father." I bow and scrape my way toward a smaller bed of coals sunk into the tatami flooring. Once they are stoked, I set a kiln onto them and set about the lengthy process of stirring the powdered green tea leaves into heated water.

Finally, I pour the boiling water into a clay teapot and set it on a wooden tray, along with teacups and a tray of tiny confections shaped like maple leaves, just like at the teahouse I'd visited once with Akiko. The raindrops against the roof high above me patter in time with the rising cadence of my heartbeat. I truly want to do a good job of presenting the shogun's representatives with tea. I am *nervous*. Where did *that* come from? God, what a strange feeling—to actually care about something. But that's the magic of playing a role; no matter how you feel about yourself, you can't let your character down.

I carry the trays to a smaller alcove, where Father and the two samurai sit with their backs to the *tokonoma* that display a scroll depicting cloudy mountain peaks and a vase holding a *chabana* of a single fresh blossom. They have removed their *katanas* and *wakizashi*, the shorter knives usually worn on the right, and placed them in front of where they kneel, parallel, like a thick demarcation line. I kneel beside Father, who faces them, and distribute the tea and sweets.

"You perform a less formal tea ceremony?" Goemon, the older samurai, asks, though he addresses my father and not me. "Well, I suppose I shouldn't expect refinement from a little village out here."

I wrinkle my nose. How complicated can it be to pour some tea?

"Thank you," the younger samurai says, with enough kindness that he seems to want to chip away at Goemon's criticism. I glance up at him and flash a grateful smile. He is a full samurai, I see now, and not just a squire like I'd originally thought. He is lean, his muscles taut without being chiseled; his eyes are the same rich dark hue of the *honjin*'s wood, clear when he looks at me, but as his gaze moves back to his senior, they bear the same smoky screen as the unpolished planks. Something in his expression tightens, and I recognize it instantly.

His look has the slow simmer of a hatred contained for too long.

I nod my head and lean back until I sit on my heels.

Goemon, the senior samurai, swallows his tea in two gulps; rather than turn the bowl deliberately in his palm to drink from a clean lip, he seems to rotate it with a tension that goes right into his shoulders. The junior samurai follows the tea ceremony protocol more closely, and nibbles at the confection with a wry grin.

Finally Goemon sets down his empty teacup. "We have been sent here to review some discrepancies in your village's records." He frowns at Father. "The shogunate is concerned your territory has not been paying its proper tithes."

Father tips his head forward before he speaks. "I would be honored to fetch the records for you. However, if you wish to rest before I do so, my daughter would be happy to show you to your rooms. You must be tired from riding, and damp from the rain—"

"We do not wish to rest. We wish to complete our work here and be done with this wretched village," Goemon says.

I rock backward. I've been so absorbed in our reenactment that I've actually forgotten to walk my path of vengeance. Now, though, I feel its old familiar hunger opening up inside of me like quicksand. I need a hatred to keep it fed. Goemon, the older samurai, seems more than happy to step up to the task. The younger man tilts his chin away with a flinch. Perhaps I'm not alone in that hate.

"Your merchants dress as well as your farmers, as if they

think themselves above their lowly station," Goemon said. "Meanwhile, your farmers behave more like their swine. You let your daughter gab in the tongue of the Western mongrels, and the stink on the streets leads me to believe you've adopted their bathing habits as well—or lack thereof." He scowls. "I can only imagine what sort of disarray the *daimyo*'s records are in."

Yodo pushes open the front door, removes her jacket and shoes, and shuffles toward us. Dark patches of rain speckle her robe and cause the loose wisps of hair against the nape of her neck to curl and frizz. "Greetings, most honorable samurai of the *bakufu*. It is an honor to host you in Kuragami village." She sinks into a kneel so deep she looks boneless as a slug. "My deepest apologies, but the *daimyo*'s clerk is not able to meet with you at this time. He has been called into the fields to settle a dispute among the farmers, but will join us as soon as it is resolved."

Goemon's silence hums in my ears: the way a forest falls too quiet just before a storm sweeps in. Then he smiles in a way that freezes my blood. Like he knows Yodo is lying, and it pleases him. As if he is hoping for a challenge. "I would like to rest after all before we explore the village," he says. "Please, show us to our rooms."

As I stand, I feel Goemon's gaze upon me, slithering down my back like a bead of sweat. Jiro, the younger samurai, waits for his senior to stand, then slides his *katana* and *wakizashi* back into his belt. "Right this way," I say, again feigning confidence that I can improvise my way out of this if I only believe hard enough that I am Miyu.

I lead them to the staircase and climb up to the second floor of the *honjin*. Instinctively, my gaze snags on the hidden panel where the museum docent told me the imperial loyalists' secret meetings were held. (Had that only been this morning? I feel like I'm fossilized in place; I can scarcely remember anything outside the rainy dome of our little role play.) My socked foot slips on a step, and I fling my arms wide to catch myself on the staircase railing. Shit. I've been too busy thinking about the hidden room.

But Jiro catches me by the wrist and holds me steady as I find my foot beneath me again. "Thank you," I say under my breath. My skin is warm where he touched me; it makes warmth bloom on my face as well.

"I hope this room is satisfactory to you." I kneel and slide open the main panel to the largest guest room. A small window on the far wall looks down on the interior garden. "If you require anything else, my room is upstairs and down the hall." The words startle me as I say them, but then, what hasn't startled me about this day?

"I am certain we will," Goemon says, and sweeps inside.

Jiro starts to follow him, but then turns to face me, and makes the slightest bow. Something hitches in my throat. "Thank you." He speaks in English. His voice twists on itself, like a ribbon of water being poured. "Your tea was . . . delicious."

I smile, though my face feels stiff, pained by it. "You're welcome," I answer in English, too. His grin goes wide.

I shuffle down the hallway before he can say anything more. The anger in my belly is still there, crackling, crackling. But it feels different from the familiar path I tread in Tokyo. It is carving a fresh path of hatred—Miyu's path. It is beating a dark new rhythm in my thoughts. However I have come to be in this role, I can't bear the thought of letting it go.

And that scares me most of all.

CHAPTER SIX

I SLIDE OPEN THE PANEL TO WHAT IS APPARENTLY MY room, step inside, and close it behind me with a heavy exhale. Silence crowds around me—no noise but the dull and distant voices of the samurai and the pattering rain. For a few moments I feel nothing, see nothing, only that murmur and drum on the roof overhead. And deep inside, I begin to feel the satisfaction of a role well played, a character I'd just pulled off.

Then Reiko's thoughts start to smother me once more.

Stupid, stupid, stupid. A Greek chorus of failures, narrating my every step. Why was I playing pretend instead of focusing on my revenge? Why get sucked into some sort of kabuki theater melodrama when I have more than enough troubles of my own? Like my brother and his shredded-up esophagus, waiting for me to give him an answer I can't possibly give. Like the RISD wait list that I've probably been struck from after the Saint Isaac's incident last winter. Like Aki and her stupid quest for indie idol fame, just begging me to put my fist right through all of her plans.

Like my quest to find the perfect revenge.

I need to cut. The need comes over me suddenly, and with a powerful undertow. Everything I've set aside while I floundered through the past hour's pageantry comes rushing back, hitting me all at once, and I desperately need to release the pressure. If I can't, I might explode.

I scan the room. Something feels lopsided about the way it is arranged, like it is an overtrimmed piece of meat. Something has been cut away. There's a low chest of drawers, a single pallet to sleep on, a wall scroll hanging on one screen depicting two women glancing behind them, smiling as they saunter down the street. A chain of *kanji* characters trails alongside the women. I move to the chest of drawers and start hunting through it. More robes, carefully wrapped around dried herbs. Blankets. A few scattered scraps of paper holding shakily written lines.

Then I find a drawer of hair accessories—combs and long metal pins. I'm shaking with relief. I pick the longest of the pins and scamper over to the pallet.

It takes far too long for me to fumble with the *obi* that holds my robe closed, then I have to dig through the starchy white robe I wear beneath the outer kimono, then unwind the strange undergarments I'm wearing beneath *that*. I bend my legs in a V, fingers trembling with anticipation. Where should I start? I run one finger along my upper thigh, already imagining how relieved I will feel to savor that pain once more—

Then I stop.

My scars are gone.

My thighs are blank. A cold, pale surface, unmarked.

No. No. Those scars were my history. My memory. How could they just be gone? The pressure swells against my eyes. Tears blur my vision as I search my stomach and hips. But there is nothing. None of the beautiful cuts I wrought the day I found out that Chloe had moved on or the day Hideki came home from Iraq for good. Who am I without my scars? Who am I without proof of my suffering?

I rip off the kimono. Hear it thunk onto the mats as the heavy stone hidden in my inner pocket strikes the floor—

And in an instant, everything changes.

❖

Someone's saying my name.

The scent of wet earth surrounds me, fresh with the possibility of growth and renewal. The rain sounds like a symphony as it filters through the trees. But here, I'm dry and warm, cradled in the hollow sanctuary, my hand resting just over the rough hewn altar where the black oddly shaped stone rests.

"Reiko." A hand curls around the sagging boulder that blocks most of the entrance to the den. "Reiko, come on. I know you don't want Aki to get drenched."

I blink, trying to place the voice. It's speaking English; that much I'm sure of, but it's much steadier than Jiro's voice, the way it rasped and twisted on itself when he spoke the foreign words. Jiro and Goemon, the shogun's representatives. Shit. Where am I? I have to get back to the *honjin*. Soon, the *daimyo*'s clerk from Kuramagi Castle will arrive from the fields, and Father will want me to—

"Reiko." Kenji squeezes around the boulder. He has to hunch his head forward to fit inside the hollow; he braces his forearm against the root-snarled roof. "Let's get back to the village and wait out the rain." He smiles, but I can see the scaffolding at the edges of it—a forced grin. "Maybe we can have some hot tea, huh, while we dry out?"

I swallow, barely able to move the muscles in my throat. Did I black out? Did I hallucinate the whole *honjin* scene? It had felt so real, even more vivid than my usual medicated anxiety trips. I could taste the scent of smoke and powdered tea leaves in the air. I can still see the way Jiro looked at me as his tongue stumbled over the English words. The "barbarian's" tongue, like Goemon said. Even at the thought of Goemon, I'm already shuddering.

"Where are they?" I ask Kenji. "Where'd the reenactors go?"

Kenji takes a step back, pressing into the grimy boulder. "The . . . uh . . . What is it, to reenact?"

"The people from the festival. They're reenacting the—" I stop. Frown. I don't like the way Kenji's looking at me. Not like I'm crazy—I know the way people look at you when they think that. They turn overly gooey, a pure sugar candy, and speak with a sunny kindergarten-teacher tone. This look is something different. Like I'm a rabid animal, and any moment, I might strike.

I'd thought it was a game for the festival. Then maybe a hallucination. Now, standing here with Kenji, I'm less sure than ever.

"We, um. We need to get Aki inside, you know, so she doesn't ruin her costume . . ."

Over his shoulder, I hear the steady percussion of rain on the tree canopy high overhead. "Sure," I say. "Sure, sure." I can explain to him once we're back in the village. (When the hell did I *leave* the village again?) I take a step toward the hollow's exit, which is enough to send Kenji squeezing back outside. But then the humming again drills into my head. I glance back at the altar, and see my silhouette glinting in the face of the curved black stone. The stone's sitting there just as it was before I picked it up. I cannot leave it behind. Whatever is happening, I know the stone is the key.

Whatever is happening . . .

I tug my hoodie sleeve down around my palm and, without touching the stone to my skin, slide it into my camera gear bag.

"Hurry *up*, Kenji," Akiko whines, as I make my way back out of the hollow. "She's going to ruin everything!"

I open my mouth to reply, but Kenji's already answering. "I think she's just having another episode. This is what your dad said to watch out for. Give her time."

Assholes. Way to talk about me like I'm not even here. I stagger back down to the trail, now gridded with mud between the old stones, and start slogging my way back toward town. Dimly, I can hear the clip-clop of Aki's wooden *geta* as she hurries to keep pace.

Just a few steps more. I grip the wooden railing as I climb the cut stone stairs onto the first tier of narrow streets. I'll find my reenactment group and we can get back to the plan. Forget Akiko and her stupid aki * LIFE * rhythm failed conglomerate. As horrible as the characters in the game were, they're far more interesting than Aki and her dumb show.

And when I was among them, I was more interesting than myself.

"Wait—Reiko, the *ryokan* is back this way—"

But the streets are empty; the only sound is the steady patter of rain. It drips into my eyes as I peer inside one of the tourist shops, where half a dozen Europeans with backpacks are crammed, pretending to look at wooden bowls and paper parasols as they wait out the downpour. No. This can't be right. The streets should be overflowing with the peasants and merchants and farmers and samurai. Where are the *daimyo*'s clerks, rushing toward the *honjin* to bring Goemon and Jiro the records they requested? Where are the merchants—the real merchants, not these tourist trap souvenir proprietors—laying out their wares for the cultural festival?

The *honjin*. I turn and charge toward the next set of stairs to take me to Kuramagi's crest. I have to get back to it. My Docs slide on the slippery stones, but I keep my grip on the railing.

"Rei, come on. What's going on?" Kenji calls behind me. "We really need to head indoors—"

But all I care about is getting back to the game. I need to slip back into Miyu's life, into her worries. Her stream of hate . . .

The *honjin* door slams shut behind me as I charge up onto the raised platform of the main room. "Excuse you!" the museum attendant cries, chasing after me. No, she's speaking Japanese—"*Sumimasen!* Your shoes! Please, you must take them off!"

But I'm already halfway up the stairs. I can't hear anything now but the throbbing of my pulse inside my ears. My skin is tightened like gooseflesh, like I'm waiting for a lightning strike. I reach Miyu's bedroom—my bedroom—and slide the rice paper panel back.

But it's been emptied out of all her things. Just a bunch of glass display cabinets, none of them from the arrangement earlier today.

"Reiko. Hey. What's the matter?" Kenji is behind me as I turn. He's too close. I slam my fists into his chest to shove him away.

"What the—hey! What'd you do that for?"

"Where are they?" I scream at him. "Where are the *hatamoto*? What happened to my costume?"

Kenji steps back from me. "Reiko . . . I'm afraid I don't understand."

What the hell is happening to me? I sink against Kenji for a moment, then pull away when he goes tense. Am I losing my mind? Overdosing on meds? Maybe I've already killed myself, I think. Maybe this is my purgatory, forever trapped with Akiko, forever going insane.

I head back downstairs, where Aki and Tadashi are arguing with the museum docent. "Please forgive my rude American cousin," Akiko is saying. "We're doing her family a favor, taking care of her. She won't be a problem much longer."

I clear my throat extra loud as I reach the downstairs, but they keep chattering away, like I'm not even there. "I know she's a clumsy oaf, but we need her help for the cultural festival. What'll it cost to repair the damage?" Tadashi asks, pulling out his wallet. "Please understand, she does not represent the aki * LIFE * rhythm brand, which is all about respect for heritage and innovation of the modern way of life . . ."

"Just get her out of here." The docent cuts her eyes toward me. "Please. Don't come back to this museum."

"The museum owner is very offended by your disregard for the museum building," Kenji says to me. Like I'm a baby. "I think we should return to the *ryokan*."

I should apologize. But I'm too tangled up in my thoughts, my panic and confusion.

I wrench my arm from Kenji's grasp and storm from the *honjin* without a word.

"She's so creepy," Mariko says behind me. "Surely you can find another photographer."

I whirl around, mouth flapping open. So Mariko's going to turn on me now, too?

"It's the only way Papa's paying for this trip. We need her." Even as Aki speaks, she forces a sour smile my way. "I don't care if we lock her in the room while we go do our real work. We just can't let Papa know."

Papa.

Then it hits me—why they're talking about me this way. Why they're talking about me honestly.

Because they're speaking Japanese.

And I understand it. As clearly as I did in the role-playing scene.

I really have lost my mind. It wasn't just a game.

As soon as we're back at Mr. Onagi's inn, I storm up to our room and grab my collection of pills. Uppers and downers. Inhibitors and relaxants. Antipsychotics. Every last one. "Reiko, what are you doing?" Aki calls to me in a singsong voice, but I don't so much as glance up at her as I head for the communal bathroom.

"Forget the weirdo," Mariko says to Aki, in Japanese. "Let's work on our project."

I kick off my slippers. Slide into my bathroom slippers— embroidered with the image of a golfer. Head to the nearest toilet.

I listen to the sounds of electronic rushing water, coming from the toilet speaker box.

And I flush down every last pill.

I grip the handrail in the handicapped stall; the hypnotic swirl of the water as it flushes is making me dizzy. I slump forward and squeeze my eyes shut. Then I remember—my scars. They had disappeared. I fumble with the button and zipper on my jeans and shove them down to expose my thighs. My scars, my wonderful marks—

They're all there, standing in a row. Dark and deep, under the skin; fresh and hot red and cracked with scabs. I haven't lost them after all. The relief hits me like a primal wind, staggers me back. I don't know what I'd do without them.

But I know they were gone, earlier. That my skin was smooth as cream.

CHAPTER SEVEN

I DON'T KNOW WHAT TO DO WITH THIS NEW SENSE of wanting inside of me.

It squeezes uncomfortably like the waistband of jeans that shrank in the dryer. (Like *all* of my clothes used to do.) It takes up room in my thoughts that I'd rather dedicate to hatred. I've lost my old familiar path, like it's been blanketed in snow and I can't distinguish it from other pathways through the trees.

I don't want to have this wanting. I don't want to feel anything. Don't want to think about anything except planning my revenge.

But it tugs at me like I'm at the end of a leash. Miyu's life was not my own—that seems abundantly clear to me now.

But wherever—whenever—Miyu's life exists, I need to get back to it. I don't know why—she certainly doesn't seem any better off than I. Her own father hates her; everyone I encountered as Miyu disrespected her. But I care about what happens to her. And this new hatred—this is a new and exciting path, and I want to walk it and wear it down.

I'm restless through the afternoon, as Akiko rehearses for the festival. Restless as Mariko types away, drafting her tragic novel on her phone. As Kenji sketches me and everyone else. I peer over his shoulder, at the gaunt figure he draws, the dark hollows in her collarbones and wells beneath her cheeks. He's made me into the spectre of death.

But now there's another world inside of me, too, and I won't let him or anyone else catch a glimpse of it.

❖

Sierra takes one look at Kenji and me sprawled on separate couches in the *ryokan*'s lounge when she arrives later in the afternoon and rolls her eyes. "You kids are pathetic." She tosses her tote bag behind the counter and flops onto the couch beside me. Unlike the rest of the inn, this room is pretty modern, with a flat-screen television and a business station and concrete walls. "What's the matter? Afraid to go out in a little rain?"

Kenji doesn't so much as glance up from the drawing he's shading. "Aki is. She's practicing in her room, so if you hear any cats screaming . . ."

Sierra grins. "Yeah, I looked up her e-store between classes this morning." Sierra squirts some hand sanitizer onto her palms and rubs it in vigorously. "Well, *your* e-store, I should say. The artwork and photographs . . . pretty amazing work."

"That's all Kenji," I say, at the same time he says, "You should see Rei's *real* work."

Sierra's eyebrows shoot up and she turns toward me. I shrink into the couch, wishing again that the earth could swallow me up like it did in my dreams last night. "I don't—" My words feel lodged in my throat, like a piece of food I can't swallow down. "I don't do real work. I'm not an . . . artist, or anything."

"Your photographs sure looked like it to me." Sierra shrugs. "The way you frame the shots, your sense of color and shadow . . ."

"Aren't they great?" Kenji says. "She should hone her talent more. I don't know why she stopped."

"Well, Kuramagi's a very scenic village. Seems like the ideal place to practice your skills."

"I don't . . ." My mouth goes dry. "No. I can't."

My head buzzes as I look from Sierra to Kenji. Why is he trying to talk me up? What does Sierra care about my art? I'm not an artist anymore. Chloe made sure of that. Maybe they're setting me up to embarrass me, just like everyone else does.

Kenji smiles back at me, like he's trying to be nice. But I don't need his kindness—or Sierra's. I don't want to be liked. I don't want to be respected. I want—I want what happened to me this morning to be real.

I know it's not. I'm not crazy. I don't know what it was, but I can't get it out of my mind.

"So." Sierra starts playing with her rings, twisting them around her fingers. One looks like a raven or crow caught mid-flight, just a silver silhouette. Another one has the Zelda Triforce logo branded into the band. "You're American. Right?"

I glance at Kenji, but if she's talking to him, he's not paying attention. He flips the page on his sketchbook and starts the broad, loose strokes of something new.

"Me? Um, yeah. Seattle born and raised." I sink farther into the couch.

"Seattle. *God.* That sounds so nice." Sierra's eyes lid, and she turns her face up, like she's basking in the warmth of some dream. "I'm from Connecticut—at least, on my mom's side. Dad's family, though, they're all military brats. Air force, navy. We lived in Okinawa for a few years before my folks got divorced." Something tugs at her smooth lips on that last word. "Guess I just couldn't stay away."

"You said you teach English, too?" I ask. Small talk always

feels like forcing my way through a thorny trail. The more I try to pull the hooks off of me, the more snag me up. I have to deflect, deflect, keep other people talking about themselves. Don't give them a chance to glimpse me at all.

"Yeah, to a bunch of bratty junior high schoolers a few towns over. They don't know I speak Japanese—don't think I know when they talk shit about me." She grins, a little bitterly. "It's easy money, but I'm pretty much always either here or there. I've been to Tokyo maybe twice in a year and a half. I think I'm ready for a new adventure."

Adventure. I try to remember how it felt a year ago, before everything went sour with Chloe, when I looked forward to something new. I look at Sierra, the soft curve of her face, her smile so confident I think she could charm open any lock. Someone who still dreams of adventure. Someone who still believes there are new worlds to see. Someone who doesn't want to sink into the dark tar of revenge and never find a way to climb out.

"Where would you go?" I ask, throat raw. "If you could go anywhere."

She crosses her arms. "Oh, anywhere, really. I'd really love to live in Manhattan, I think, but travel a lot. Learn even more languages, boss people around. I just always want to experience something new. There's too much of the world out there for us not to live it, you know?" she asks, looking right at me.

I don't know. Before today, I didn't want to experience

anything ever again. But now I know Miyu. With all my familiar hatreds in a new puzzle, it feels like a first step.

Like maybe I can actually see it through.

"Well, anyway." She looks away; only as she does so do I realize she's deflating a little, like I've let her down. Well, welcome to life with Reiko. "My favorite show's coming on. Stick around if you want—I'll translate for you," she adds with a grin.

"Oh, you'll like this show," Kenji says, eyes flickering from his sketchbook to the screen and back. "Right up your alley."

He's actually right—it's an anime show about a kid who finds a notebook of names, and anytime he writes someone's name in it, it makes them die. *Deathnote*, Sierra translates, though I understand the Japanese far better than I have any right to. What I wouldn't give to have a book like that for myself. The names I'd write in it—Chloe and Hideki and my parents and half of the Saint Isaac's students and administrators; Akiko and Mariko, too. And then, once I'd witnessed every last one of their deaths, gloated over their graves, I'd write my name in the book and be on my way.

After the show is over and Sierra leaves, I ask Kenji what he was sketching. He's depicted Sierra and me on the couch—her all brightness and bronze, loose, luxurious lines. But I'm shadow and iron, a thick-pressed hatch mark of darkness that sucks the life right out of the page. Well, maybe that is Reiko, a dense dead star collapsing in on herself. But I imagine Miyu as the white space around the sketch—a fresh, empty expanse for me to slip into.

"She likes you," Kenji tells me, a faint grin on his face. "Sierra."

I narrow my eyes. He's wrong. And even if he weren't—I can't. I'm here for one thing only. Revenge. Yet my eye keeps tracing that white space. I can almost feel Miyu's life surrounding me again, pulling me in. I wonder if I can return to it.

"Come on." I slide off the couch. "Let's eat."

I'm ravenous tonight. At dinner I swallow down every bowl of tempura set before me, even the crunchy fried fish bones.

"Are we going out again tonight?" Mariko asks while I inhale my food.

"There's nothing better to do," Aki says with a shrug. But then her gaze narrows; she peers at Mariko from the side. "What's it to you?"

Mariko tugs her sweater sleeves down over her hands and ducks her head. "Well, I—I thought maybe we'd see those guys again. The ones who bought us the free drinks—"

"Hatoshi. You like Hatoshi," Aki says. Mariko's cheeks go dark and she nods. "Don't be ridiculous. He's so far out of your league. You're better off with Junmei—the shorter one, remember? He seems like the kind of *otaku* who'd actually read a cell phone novel."

"Oh." Mariko sets down her chopsticks. "Oh—yeah, you're right. He was all right, too."

I no longer have room for pity inside of me. Mariko is worse than Aki. If she wants to snap toward Aki's whims like a rubber band, who am I to feel sorry for her?

"That club sucked. Not nearly enough cute girls," Kazuo says. "Aside from Aki, of course."

Aki makes a show of rolling her eyes, but then both she and Kazuo glance toward Tadashi; he's busy punching something into his phone. "They aren't too bad. But they need my help. The aki * LIFE * rhythm brand. Let's hand out cards this time. Direct them to the site." Aki shoves away her barely touched plate of tempura. "Did we get any traffic bumps from last night?"

"Not a huge bump, but it's a start. Any luck on that interview, Tadashi?" Kazuo asks.

Tadashi holds up one hand and continues typing.

I hate you all, I want to say. *I hope you claw each other's eyes out. Keep causing one another pain. You all deserve it. And so much more.*

I stagger to my feet. "Have fun," I tell the table. My head's buzzing. A smile crosses my face, but I don't quite know why.

"Reiko?" Kenji asks. "Are you feeling all right?"

"Just a little tired," I say. A total lie. I could scale the far mountain's peak right now. I could leap from the *ryokan*'s roof and soar.

I need to get back to Miyu's life. The want inside of me is digging, digging in. I exit the dining room and slide the panel door shut behind me with such force it makes a sound like a rifle crack. I stalk down the polished wood hall of the dining wing, barely glancing out the row of windows that look onto the inner courtyard. I nearly slam into Sierra as she carries a tray of desserts toward another dining room.

"Careful!" she cries, catching herself at the last minute.

I don't reply. I'm on a warpath for our upstairs room. The pressure in my head intensifies. I slide open the door and head to my camera, which I had tossed on my bed.

When I pick up the camera bag, I see it. The stone I'd taken from the altar. I can't believe I left it up here while I was downstairs all day.

It gleams like something cold and condensed, nestled in a compartment of the bag. It looks like my hatred, compressed and fossilized. My heart settles into a steady resting beat as I dump the stone out onto my pallet, admiring the irregular shape. It's like a comet, curving toward itself. A double-sided weapon—stabbing on one end and bludgeoning on the other.

For the second time today, I pick up the stone.

It nestles so neatly in my palm, the heavy round end in the meat of my hand while the tip curls up toward the base of my fingers. I barely have time to settle under the covers before it tugs me under, the drumbeat of my heart rattling under my skin—

❖

I stand in a garden, on a covered walkway just outside the paneled walls. Water trickles down a slope of rocks at one end of the garden, pooling beneath a well-pruned ancient tree that curves, sheltering, over the pond. The sound of rushing water weaves together with a faint, chiming breeze until I can almost believe I am the only person alive in the world, and that the whole world is contained within these garden walls.

I recognize this place: the interior courtyard of the *honjin*. I pad around for the hidden pockets of my kimono, which opens just beneath the *obi* wound around my waist. Sure enough, the stone is tucked inside.

Relief and confusion clash within me. Yes, I want to be back here, but I still don't understand how this can be. It seems too elaborate to be a hallucination or a dream. I haven't stumbled on some reenactment for the cultural festival. Somehow, the stone is the key—it brought me to this world. *Don't lose the stone, Reiko,* I chide myself.

No—that isn't quite right. I'm not Reiko anymore.

I am Miyu.

The world smells damp and freshly scrubbed from a hard rain, though I no longer hear the gentle patter of raindrops against the pond and the walkway's roof. On the far side of the mountain valley, a dull, cloud-screened sun throbs and slices itself on the mountains' edge. I move down the walkway onto the garden's thick carpet of grass and stand for a moment, inhaling the wonderful scents. Then I glance up at the *honjin*. On the second floor, a silhouette against the window moves and backs away.

Jiro and Goemon's room. My face goes warm, and I hurry back inside.

As soon as I slide the panel door closed, the aroma of sizzling meat washes over me. Yodo hunches over the cauldron in the center of the great room, preparing skewers. "Miyu!" she calls out, as soon as she catches sight of me. "Make yourself useful, impudent girl. Fetch us some herbs for the soup."

For a moment, hatred spikes through me, like a pinched nerve, but it also feels comforting. *"Hai, Yodo-in."* I bow at the waist and leave my sandals at the door. I will not complain. This is where I wanted to be—in Miyu's life. No ghost Chloe and Hideki and all the rest lurking just over my shoulder. No aki * LIFE * rhythm to peddle and perfect.

All the simple acts of Miyu's daily life—finding the herb basket, donning my jacket—come to me so easily it is like

I've always known them. I sling a woven basket into the crook of my arm and head for the streets of Kuramagi.

I thought I had a decent sense of Kuramagi's layout, but the subtle changes between this Kuramagi and the one I walked through this morning with Aki and the team are more disorienting than helpful. All the buildings look the same—a little grimier and more soot-stained, but otherwise, they are all where they belong with blue-and-white banners flapping in the breeze. It is the contents that confuse me—the tiny shop that sold funky ice-cream flavors (charcoal, green tea, chestnut) this morning is now a butcher's shop, and a leathery old woman stands out front swatting a pig's carcass with a towel to scatter flies. All the souvenir shops have faded into cloistered stands of indeterminate goods.

As I walk down the street, I feel a strange magnetic push parting the crowds away from me. One man, a farmer with his hands soiled from the rice paddies, tugs his son up by the arm and steers him far from my path. Another little girl ducks her head at the sight of me and scampers to the other side of the street. A woman leans against her store's wooden column curling her lip back and staring at me like a vicious crow.

None of them say a word, but they don't need to. The buzzing in my head swells and pops, and all the names they call me come gushing out: *impure girl, fool, harlot, disgrace*.

My throat constricts. What have I done to offend them so? *No*, I remind myself harshly. What has *Miyu* done? Are we one and the same? Chloe used to ramble at length about reincarnation and past lives—am I living one now?

I grasp for any memories, any clues as to why the townspeople are reacting to me this way, why I am so certain it is really me who is the target of their hate. Why can I remember only tiny details, nothing significant? Miyu's life is like a puzzle being doled out to me piece by piece, the next one not available until I've snapped the previous one into the right place. When I try to remember who these villagers are, all I hear are the echoes of old words they've said to me, tossed out like slop from a cistern. *Shameful. Idiot. Cursed.*

I clutch the basket to my chest, cradling it like a child, and hurry down to the herbalist's shop.

The herbalist is a prime example of the merchants who populate Kuramagi—the lowest caste, greedy and incapable of real work. Or so Father always says. (When he told me so, I don't know, but like most clues, it seems to come to me as a matter of course.) He wears a dark men's kimono, its hem frayed and muddy, and smells like he hasn't bathed in some time. Brown nicotine stains spread across his fingers and his teeth as he leers at me.

"What brings a wretch like you to me?" he asks, leaning over his counter. "Don't suppose you're looking to make a trade."

The way his stare sears across my flesh leaves no doubt in my mind about what sort of trade he means. I glare right back at him.

"Oh, don't look so coy. Everyone knows what you're like. What your worth is. Your papa may have the *daimyo* fooled, but he'll know he's buying damaged goods soon enough." He bares a toothy grin. "Your goods are valid to me, though. I'm not picky."

"I have nothing to sell to you," I snap. "I just want some tea, some scallions, a package of sesame seeds. Dried mushrooms, if you have any."

"It's not a good season for them. It might cost you," he says.

I grind my teeth together. "You can put it on my father's tab."

He stares at me a moment longer, then eases back from the counter. "You should get off your high horse," he says as he starts assembling my purchases. "A failed *Ohatsu*. You're no good to anyone now."

"Fortunately, I don't need anyone." I snatch the bundle of herbs from him and stuff it into my basket, then turn precariously on my wooden sandals and totter away.

Misplaced shame burns hot on my face. I imagine the stray raindrops sizzling against my skin. What do I have to be ashamed of? What has Miyu done that is so terrible? The merchant seems to imply her purity had been compromised—an archaic concept that almost makes me laugh out loud, right in the middle of the street—but there seems to be more to it than that.

I try wracking my memory for clues. If some useful

tidbits of knowledge come to me right at the moment I need them—like speaking Japanese, for starters, or understanding the complex system of ranks and caste and where I fit in it—then maybe if I concentrate I can dig deeper, find out more than just the most immediate information.

I try to focus, clear my mind, search for memories, but it doesn't seem to work. It's as if a steel door is blocking me from accessing my own mind.

As I avoid yet another woman's stare on the street, I dart my free hand into my pocket and clench a fist around the stone. The woman ducks beneath a strand of the lightning-shaped paper *shide* that marks the entrance to a shrine. I don't need any spirits to protect me. My fingers rub back and forth against the stone's smooth surface. I have myself for protection. That's all I need.

The stone warms under my touch, like a living, breathing thing. As if it's my touch that brings me here, that pulls me into its gravity. I imagine that I am inside a bubble, where no sound can reach me. The silence buzzes in my ears, a comforting blanket of noiseless noise.

CHAPTER EIGHT

I DROP OFF THE HERBS WITH YODO IN THE KITCHEN and set about helping her dish up a meal for the samurai. She drapes two small river trout across heated stones and waits for the sizzle of the fish to fill the room.

"You prepared the upstairs for your father's guests?" she asks me, her tone low and urgent.

The upstairs? I have a feeling she means the secret room and not the room where Goemon and Jiro are staying. "It's ready," I find myself answering.

Yodo manages a tight, bitter smile as she churns the pot of rice. "Well, at least you aren't completely useless."

"A minor miracle," I agree. Just to see what she'll say. Has Miyu ever tried to counter her bullies before? Or does she slink away from their insults with the same urge I've felt in the streets?

Yodo tilts her head to one side; the loose bun on top of her head slides precariously as she does so. She reminds me of Hideki's old cat, a grumpy, furry blob that hated any and all human interaction, with one exception—it could never turn down a fake catnip mouse to toy with. Finally, Yodo chuckles to herself. "You're a strange one, Miyu." She presses a pair of soup bowls into my hands. "Just don't be strange around the *hatamoto*."

The rest of the evening is a blur of hauling dozens of tiny dishes between the kitchen and the private dining enclave where Goemon and Jiro sit. Goemon's toad-like expression rumples further each time I appear and kneel down before them, but Jiro smiles and bids me to wait while they eat the latest dish of raw fish or roasted fish or stewed vegetables or rice.

"Have you spent much time beyond Kuramagi?" he asks me, taking care to set his chopsticks down flat atop his bowl rather than skewering them upright.

I glance at Goemon first; I don't want to draw his ire if he feels, like my father seems to feel, that girls like me are to be seen and not heard. But he is busy slurping down his udon noodles. "A bit, your lordship."

Like, eighteen years away from here, I think.

"I'd like to see more of the world someday," Jiro says. That earns him an arch glance from Goemon. "Later, of course. Perhaps if the shogun chooses to accept the trade offers of the foreigners." Jiro loops a noodle around his chopstick. "I could serve as an ambassador to China, or America, or France."

"We've gotten on just fine for hundreds of years without the barbarians' trade," Goemon says. "I see no reason to start."

But Jiro is watching me; I feel his gaze on the bared skin at the nape of my neck like a warm ember. Have I worn my kimono too low in the back? Modesty dictates the collar be high up against my neck, like a pious Confucian woman. But Miyu does not seem inclined to worry about such things. "Perhaps it is your lack of experience with other cultures that prevents you from seeing their value," Jiro says to Goemon. But he is smiling right at me, something dark in his grin. It comforts me. I know that darkness, too. "Not everyone ascribes to the same code as we do. I find it fascinating to learn how others live."

"Well, here, we follow whatever code the shogun requires of us." Goemon holds his empty bowl out to me. "Fetch me more."

I offer him my sweetest smile and rise to bring him another round of noodles.

Why am I so intrigued by this life? I am treated about the same here as I am treated by Aki and her crew. Perhaps worse, given the open hostility I've encountered from people I don't even know. In my normal life, I usually have to at least

open my mouth to get people to hate me—from my ignorance of customs to my classmates back home who find me
awkward, stilted, strange. I feel a certain grace as Miyu.
The same wit I've displayed as an elven sorceress on the
Legends of Eldritch Journey role-playing game forums shines
through in this role as well, though I never can seem to use it
as myself.

Maybe it is the anonymity—the sense that I am not myself. Like posting an anonymous, hateful comment on the
internet, or wearing a mask. I am uninhibited as Miyu. People
expect me to be sour and hateful, and so pay me no mind.
Here there's no Kenji around to chide me or Hideki to taunt
me with guilt. As Miyu, my hatred can run free.

"You move slower than an ox," Goemon grumbles, when I
return with his bowl.

"My apologies, your lordship." I kneel so low my forehead
grazes the floor. "The cook is not young, you see."

Goemon stuffs a chopstickful of noodles into his mouth
and speaks around them. "A whole village of buffoons. Why
did the shogun send us to this damned place again?"

Jiro catches my gaze for a splintered second before looking
back to Goemon. "To review the *daimyo*'s records, of course—"

"Quiet, boy. I know why." Goemon swallows. "At least tell
me there's a decent tavern nearby with a good supply of sake."
He gestures to his full cup. "This one tastes like rice farmer's
piss."

I start to scoop their plates up into my arms. "There is a lovely tavern on the lower level of the town, *dono-sama*. Just a few blocks to the north. I am sure you will find the company and drink there to your tastes."

"Wonderful. Come, Jiro, let's go. Maybe something in this town is worth the hassle."

Jiro reaches for his *wakizashi* and tucks it into his sash. "Actually, I . . ." He lowers his head. "I thought I might get some rest."

Goemon studies him for a moment. Propriety tells me I should leave now; leave the master and student to their little spat. But I feel compelled to stand by, to silently cheer Jiro on.

That is a mistake.

"Ahh," Goemon says softly, and there is no missing the harsh scrape of his gaze across me. "Yes, of course you do. Very well. Just don't forget what we've come for." His voice lowers on that last. "Don't forget your oaths."

Goemon rises, mats creaking beneath his bare feet, and returns his weapons to his sash. Once more he studies me with a slimy smile on his face as he walks past me for the *honjin* entrance. I shudder, dishes rattling in my arms.

"I'm sorry about him," Jiro says, as soon as his master departs. "But men like him always reap the poisoned harvest they sow."

"You think so?" I ask. I want it to be true, but I have my doubts.

"I know it."

I meet his gaze, my arms tingling. Again I hear the drum-beats, ringing through my thoughts. Vengeance. Perhaps Jiro follows their rhythm, too.

The moment passes, and he softens his expression. "Do you . . . would you like any help?"

I know he is only trying to be polite. But I shake my head. "No, your lordship. It is my pleasure to serve." My father's words taste vile in my mouth, but I smile all the same. Before Jiro has a chance to respond, I head for the kitchen.

Father is in an unfiltered, pinpricked rage over the samurai as soon as I enter. A tight pain in my gut tells me I ought to steer clear, but for once, his anger doesn't appear to be directed at me. I dump the dishes into the washing basin and keep my head down to avoid his stare.

"The gall of that man. What a disgrace." He whirls around the kitchen, clenching and unclenching his fists. "Samurai these days are nothing but glorified clerks. Their oaths mean nothing. And what of the *bushido*? The whole vulgar system is teetering over the edge."

"You should be glad for his idiocy," Yodo says. "If he had a hair of sense on his head, he'd sniff us out for sure."

I sit up straighter at that, washrag going still. What scheming is she afraid the *hatamoto* will sniff out?

"Don't be so sure that they haven't. Their timing couldn't be worse." Father snatches a pan from Yodo's hands. "Why would they choose the festival day, of all days, to conduct this ridiculous review? When they know everything will be in an upheaval and out of sorts. It makes no sense—unless they've been warned in advance of our plans."

"And who would warn them? The *daimyo*?" Yodo asks, then snorts.

They are afraid their conspiracy has been discovered, but they don't know they aren't the only village plotting against the shogunate. That's what the docent at the *honjin* told me, anyway. I drop the pot I am scrubbing back into the washbasin with a weighty thud. "You're both blind," I say. "Convinced there are screens upon screens trying to shield you from the truth."

My gut twists on itself. Memories ripple through me, puzzle pieces suddenly coming all at once, piling up against each other until I can no longer tell one from the next. "The samurai are here as a precautionary measure. After the attempted rebellions against the shogunate in Mito and Choshue, they are taking no risks." When did I learn about the rebellions in Mito and Choshue? Another puzzle piece, offered up to me from nothingness. "They do not suspect you yet, but they are here to prevent exactly what you aim to do. Give them any reason to be suspicious, and they will find it. They'll stop you."

Father has ceased his restless movements; he and Yodo watch me like they expect something more to happen. I am shaking. Worn out from saying so much, from drawing on so many memories, all the ones necessary to pull together even that short statement.

But I am confident in my words. I know I heard snatches of conversations about the constant tug of war between the shogun and the emperor's supporters—I know my father and his friends at the *daimyo*'s estate fall into the latter camp. I remember watching not only the shogun's bannermen like Goemon and Jiro sweep through town, but also worse men than them. Men who demanded fealty to the shogunate. I worked hard to avoid such men; I learned how to carry myself to escape their notice. Others in the village were not so fortunate.

"You think you are so clever," Father says, voice raspy and low, "that you can puzzle out things others can't. But you miss what's right in front of you." He turns from me with a grunt. "You are dismissed."

I gather up my robe's hem. What is right in front of Miyu? I wish I knew.

Who are you, Miyu? I ask. *What have you suffered through?*

But I am only asking myself, it seems. There is no one else around to answer me.

CHAPTER NINE

FATHER'S CO-CONSPIRATORS ARRIVE IN SILENCE, mist sweeping into the back door on their robes' skirts and coiling at our feet as I admit them. They make no eye contact with me and speak no words; I stand back and let them guide themselves to the panel at the top of the back stairs. I'm quite certain that whatever they're planning, I'm not invited to take part.

I go to my room, but I still can't shake the sense that there's something wrong here—that it is missing a vital organ, that it is lopsided, somehow. I dig through my drawers and unearth a poetry book and a few other personal effects, but half of the drawers have been emptied out. Very strange.

I flop down onto my pallet, but don't feel the slightest tug of sleep.

I am, as far as I can tell, in Edo-period Japan. And I am . . . bored.

I pull the stone from my pocket and turn it slowly in my hand. Is this the key to returning to my own life? I consider testing it, but I'm not sure I'm ready to go back yet. The only thing awaiting me is a night out with Aki and her friends at a stupid club. Or maybe I can find myself a fresh razor and start a new network of scars.

But I no longer feel like a water balloon stretched too tight, needing to burst open with pain. And I certainly want nothing to do with Akiko. Not now that I can hear how everyone really feels. And I can't stand the way Kenji and Sierra prod at me, like if they tug on the right string, I might have something worthwhile to say.

I snatch the poetry book and head back to the garden, where I started out this trip.

A sour wind blows through the night, carrying the heavy scent of dying leaves up from the valley. I light the candles in a few paper lanterns along the walkway, though once I close the rice paper panels, the soft amber light glowing through the paper gives me light enough to read. I perch on the walkway's edge, feet dangling over the grass, and open the book, flipping to the first poem.

I abruptly stop.

Oh, what the *hell*? The Japanese characters float on the page in front of me, but I can't read them? In this world, I can understand Japanese but not read it. I squint at the characters. No, I'm mistaken—I can read some of it. The syllables in *hiragana*, and a few of the *katakana* ones besides. But all of the pictograms borrowed from Chinese, the *kanji*, remain dense, incomprehensible blocks of dashes and bars.

I plop the book into my lap and lean back. Well, of course. Women weren't taught *kanji* in the Edo period. I groan— probably something else a proper Confucian woman isn't supposed to do.

The wall panel behind me slides open. I scramble to sit up straight so quickly that the book tumbles out of my lap and lands in the garden below. "Oh!" Jiro cries. "I'm so sorry. I didn't mean to—to startle you—"

"It's not your fault." I reach for my wooden sandals, sitting beside me on the walkway ledge. "I'm the one lurking out here in the half-dark."

He grins at that, then holds out his hand to halt me. "No, don't get up. Let me fetch it for you." He trots down into the garden and plucks my book up from the grass. "Poetry. You can read this?" he asks. His tone is light, flickering with wonder, perhaps; I feel sure he doesn't mean offense. Still, his words sting, and I glance away from him.

"I'm sorry. I—I didn't mean—" he says.

"It's all right." I force a smile. "Unless, of course, you're the one who wrote the law."

He laughs, a raspy sound like the rattling of bare branches. "Trust me," he says, "I don't hold that kind of power in the *bakufu*." He hands the book back to me. "I'm sorry as well, though, for the way my master treated you earlier. He is . . ." Jiro hesitates, and I see again that tension in his face. "He is not always an honorable man."

"I'm used to far worse."

Jiro's smile looks like it aches. He hops onto the walkway and sits as well, leaving enough distance between us for propriety. "It wasn't always like this, you know. I've heard about the old days in some of the epics, like *The Tale of the Heike*. Back before the shogunate came to power, men and women were regarded as equals. Your sex could own property, manage affairs, educate yourselves however you chose. It's only in the past few hundred years that we've turned away from that. That we've let ourselves become so rigid."

"Why the change?" I ask.

Jiro thinks for a moment. "Some of the men in the *bakufu* credit the influence of our trade with the Chinese. Of course, they see it as a good thing that we've hardened into the rigid structure that we have now . . . And yet, do you know what's one of the first things they teach us, when they train us to wield the *katana*?" he asked.

I shake my head. "Don't grip it by the blade?" I guess.

Jiro stares at me for a minute, then breaks into a grin. "That would be a good place to start, wouldn't it?" He leans back against the wooden post of the walkway. "No. They teach us about how the blade is shaped. A sheet of steel, folded over itself dozens and dozens of times. But it isn't perfectly rigid. It has to be able to bend and flex. Otherwise, it will snap clean off the moment you try to pierce with it."

"Because it's too brittle," I say. "And you think our life under the shogunate is much the same."

"It's already happening." His gaze drifts off toward the mountain peaks. "We're already fracturing into a dozen shards. Some people want the shogunate gone and the emperor returned. Some want to remove the emperor. Some want to trade with the foreigners, others, to kill them all—*sonno joi*—death to the barbarians, all that rot. Some say we should go to the foreign lands ourselves and conquer them, others, that we should keep to ourselves . . ."

As he lists all these conflicting factions, each plucks like a muffled chord inside me. A distant familiarity. I know these things, but how I learned them, I couldn't say. Was it through Miyu? Through whatever bits and pieces of history I'd managed to accumulate as Reiko? After all, I know how the conflict between the emperor and shogun turns out.

What would happen if I gave it away? I don't want to be responsible for altering the course of history, certainly. It hadn't even occurred to me—is that why I've come to the past? To change its fate?

Don't be an idiot, Reiko. You can't change the world. I clench my teeth; it is the truth. I am a nothing girl, a no one, a weed in the cracks of time. But maybe as Miyu, I do have the chance to be someone. If I have the power to become someone powerful. Someone truly in control.

I take a deep breath and steady myself. "You're the samurai. The front lines—the shogun's sword. What is it that you think should happen?" I ask Jiro.

Jiro laughs his hollow, rattling laugh again. "That doesn't mean much anymore, either. Do you know?" He pops the hilt of his *katana* so that I can see a few fingers' width of blade glinting in the lantern light. "I've never even used this in real combat. Only training exercises. Drills. I sit at a desk all day back in Kyoto. I review records and talk to all the other useless *bakufu* men. The shogunate has brought peace, yes, but back before the shogunate, we had a real purpose."

"Sure," I say. "Because there was more violence. More upheaval."

Jiro's gaze turns brittle. "Maybe that's the price of progress. Of taking risks. Friction is a natural part of change. Now we have . . . nothing. We stagnate, and float along. Violence isn't inherently evil. It's part of nature," he says. "Restorative. Cleansing."

I hold my breath, letting it burn in my lungs. A dangerous feeling creeps over me when I look at him, a feeling like when I'm making a new cut on the inside of my thigh.

"Cleansing. Like a forest fire," I say.

"Yes." Jiro smiles softly. "Like that."

We both fall silent. I study Jiro—the soft, short lashes that frame his eyes and the subtle slope of his cheeks. The way his nimble fingers play along the diamond pattern on the hilt of his sword. He seems content for now, but with a restlessness beneath it. Maybe he itches to use that sword one day, if he finds a cause righteous enough. He is seeking a purpose.

I gesture toward the book sitting between us. "Would you . . . could you read me some of the poetry?"

Jiro's cheeks darken; he looks like he is fighting back a grin. "Of course I could. But I—I mean, I'm no actor—"

"You don't have to be. I just want to hear the sounds and words. I'm trying to . . . to understand the world around me better." *To decide if this world really suits me*, I think, though I can't explain that to him. To decide if the possibilities of Miyu's life are worth continuing Reiko's life for a little bit longer.

"Yes. Yes, of course." Jiro flips through the pages while he clears his throat. "Gracious. This is not the best collection . . . Well, here we go."

He sits up straight and stares hard down into the book.

The three friends of winter—
Bamboo, plum, and pine.
The wind, cold and bitter,
But inside, warm and ripe.
Plum to warm our bellies,
Pine to shield from snow.
Bamboo to support us,
As skin begins to glow.

Both my eyebrows shoot up. Jiro's cheeks look as warm as embers.

Your warmth holds me closely,
Your breath beats my heart.
The three friends of winter
Shelter us from harm.

My skin tingles as his words rippled over me. His voice is cool and flowing, cascading like a waterfall, breaking only as embarrassment trips him up. But he is earnest as he speaks. Enraptured with the words, even if they are a little cheesy. I wonder if I can even explain cheesiness, as a concept, to a nineteenth-century samurai.

"Well," I say. "I, ah . . . I take it that was written by a man, seeing as how a woman would probably get scorned to no end for speaking so frankly."

"Yes. Yes, it was." His whole face is a deep shade of scarlet now. "Actually, ah . . . that's one of my own works."

The wind rushes out of me. A poet philosopher samurai? Maybe we are both people out of time, destined for another life to take as our own. He certainly doesn't belong to this rigid world. "It's—it's lovely."

"You don't have to say that," he starts.

"No, really, it is. It's honest and gentle, and . . ." I pause with a faint twinge in my heart. "It must have been about someone truly special to you."

"I thought so, at the time." His words curl inward on himself, though he glances away. "It turned out she did not share the sentiment."

I remember the look on Chloe's girlfriend's face when she opened the door to me. Chloe shouting for her in the background, then her face going white as bone as she peered past the doorway to where I stood. The rage inside me was a monster, another creature, something trying to escape. The anger feels as fresh now as it did the day it happened. I feel the same urge to put my fist through something. To break the world around me.

The urge to break myself came later. It's what happens when the anger can't get free. Looking at the taut muscles of Jiro's neck, the whitened knuckles around his sword's hilt, I wonder if he feels the same thing. The same need to break free.

"Tell me another one," I say, turning toward him. I tuck my legs under me. "One that's not about . . . her."

It takes him a moment to bring himself back to me. From the darkened expression on his face, I know he's left something of himself in the past memory. But then he smiles again. Studies me. And closes his eyes.

A flower bud is a sealed world, unknown, packed with
    possibility.
What color will it be when it unfurls? What secrets will
    it expose?
What fragrance will it leave upon my hands, lingering
    through my day and echoing in my dreams?

"I think I like that one much better," I say.

"Are you certain?" He props his chin in one hand. "I only wrote it earlier today. It still needs some altering."

My heartbeat rises in my ears.

"It's not a very fitting hobby for a warrior, I realize," he says.

I smirk. "Well, you said yourself you're not much of a warrior, either."

Jiro laughs fully at that. I like his real laugh—rich and earthy, not the dried-out sad little laugh he made before. "Not by choice!"

"At least you chose poetry," I say. "At least you continue

with it, regardless." My own past hobbies stung and I wasn't strong enough to continue them. I feel the absence of the art I'll never make and the photos I'll never splice together like a missing tooth. "I . . . I used to paint."

Now it's Jiro's turn to raise both eyebrows. "Really? That's very impressive—more so than my silly words. Why did you stop?"

"It wasn't proper for a girl." I think of Jiro and his swords; Jiro and his wish for battles bygone. "They . . . other people didn't like what I chose to portray."

He cants his head to one side. "Why? What did you paint?"

I remember the black-and-white photographs glued to the canvases. The class picture heads detached from their shoulders, the cheerleaders' legs heaped in a pyramid. The magazine cutouts and printouts from the internet of guns and knives and burning effigies. My grin comes from somewhere deep inside of me, painted on with a thick brush, dipped in red. "Violence," I say. My voice is molten; it makes me glisten from within. "Upheaval. Renewal."

Jiro meets my gaze from the corner of his eyes. "Progress," he says slowly.

I nod. The pounding in my heart has turned to thunder, and my skin crackles like lightning strikes.

"You know, Miyu . . ." He hesitates, and clutches the poetry book, fingers running along its edges. "I could teach you to read the *kanji*. If you wished."

I meet his gaze.

"Then you could read all the poetry you liked. You wouldn't have to rely on me and my poor recitation."

"Nonsense. You recite wonderfully," I say. "But . . . but yes. I'd like that very much."

His grin splits his face in two. "There are books I don't have memorized." He looks sheepish; hesitant. As if he knows he is speaking heresy. "Unusual books. Ones that I think you might find fascinating, once you're able to read them."

Finally, I catch his meaning. He's talking about forbidden texts—ones that challenge the shogunate, perhaps, or at least the status quo. Dangerous ideas that have been locked away. Maybe he's even been forced to try to stamp out those ideas, once. *Violence. Upheaval. Renewal.* The three words play a new chord in my heart. "I—I think I'd like that very much."

Jiro beckons me over to him. I slide across the wooden walkway and nestle beside him, our thighs nearly touching, the book open between us. He flips through the poetry book, squinting, then flattens out a page toward the front. "Here we are. One of the easiest ones—*mountain. San.* See how it looks like a range?"

It looks like a trident to me, but I suppose I could see it as a mountain range, as well.

"And then river. *Sen.* These three lines, like a stream rushing past."

He coaches me through a dozen or so of the simplest

characters. *Moon* and *day, woods, earth, wind.* I point to one with a triangular roof that seems to be swinging two parcels back and forth, like scales. "What's this one?"

Jiro smiles again. *"Fate."*

Fate. I've never believed in fate. Maybe briefly, when Chloe's juicy mouth first crashed into mine, I tried to believe that there was a plan for me. That I wasn't forever doomed to loneliness and Hideki's cruelty. But now I have no fate. No future. No purpose.

At least, Reiko doesn't.

But maybe Miyu could.

The lights in the house on the other side of the gardens snuff out; overhead, the sky is a deep indigo wash, speckled with thousands of stars. I forgot how beautiful the world can be when you get far enough away from other people, when you clear all of their junk out of the way. I imagine that starlight washing over me.

Jiro taps two fingers against the back of my palm. "I'm sorry, Miyu," he says. "I didn't mean to keep you out here so late."

"Why be sorry? It's the most interesting conversation I've had all week," I say.

Jiro's fingers brush against the top of my hand again, hovering, as if he were trying to decide something. Finally, he clenches his hand into a fist and stands. "I'll have to try harder next time," he says. "See if I can make it the best of the month."

I laugh despite myself. "Something to aspire toward." I stand as well; my kimono's hem falling heavy against the wooden planks. "Good night, Jiro-sama." I kneel to him before backing away. "If you require anything for your stay, you . . . well." I smile. "You know where to find me."

"And you know where to find me," he says.

The garden air thickens between us. Warmth cuts through the autumn night. For the first time in months, I imagine how it might feel to close that gap—to feel arms wrapped around me again and fingers in my hair. Ones that don't belong to Chloe. Ones that I don't have to imagine in my head, coaxed out of the text on a screen from my internet boyfriend on the Legends of Eldritch Journey RPG forums. But it is a useless dream. I can't go flinging myself at some samurai I've only just met. What could Jiro even want with me?

"Good night, Miyu," he says. His shoulders fall, and I turn and slide open the screen.

CHAPTER TEN

AS I AM COMING UP THE STAIRCASE, FATHER PASSES me on his way down. His meeting is all finished, then. His features are contorted, keyed up by whatever he and his friends have discussed; he beckons me to follow him into the thick-walled kitchens.

"Where have you been?" Father hisses, packing a lot of force into his quiet words.

I stand up straight. "Distracting the samurai. Like you asked me to," I add, just now remembering a conversation I'm not certain I'd been present for.

Father frowns. "I thought they went to the tavern. Drink themselves away for the night."

"The older one did. Jiro—ahh, the younger one remained

here." I raise my eyebrows. "I thought you might appreciate my aid, since you aren't watching out so closely for yourself."

Father slaps the back of my hand. I rear back, more out of shock than pain; the sleeves of my kimono fall forward to cover the bared skin he touched. He moved so fast, and yet he was careful. He's hurt me this way before, where no one can see the marks.

"Do what you must to keep them busy," he says finally. "But don't get too cozy. Remember—I'm selling you to Tsurube as soon as his *sankin kotai* concludes."

While I have no idea what a Tsurube or a *sankin kotai* are, I understand the message all too clearly. I am property. I swallow hard and circle around my father toward the kitchen exit. Even in Miyu's body, I will never truly be free.

Upstairs, I sit in Miyu's bedroom for several minutes, legs curled under me on the pallet, and try to sort out my thoughts. I can make Father pay. He wants to sell me off to someone named Tsurube? I can make the price far too steep. Or make myself worthless to Father. A dark image flashes through me—a knife in my hand, stolen from the samurai, perhaps, carving deep gashes in my face. I wonder what the *kanji* for *freedom* is. The *kanji* for *rage*.

But no good solution comes to me. The cavernous room, half-empty, echoes around me with nothing but my own racing thoughts. Half-empty. I stare through the grayish dark.

That's what is wrong with the room.

I am meant to share it with someone else.

Whom had I lost? A sibling? A husband? The villagers treat me like a traitor, like someone who's committed some horrible crime. But that can't be true. If I'd really done something so dishonorable, I'd be dead, or imprisoned. Like Jiro said, women had no freedom, no rights—any crime I might have perpetrated would have sent me far from here.

I pull the stone from my pocket. The stone seems to be the key for moving between this life and my own. If I can go back to my time, maybe I can find more answers for Miyu there. Maybe if the stone is the key, I can use it to gain more control. I look at the stone in my fist. I pry one finger away, then another . . .

The moment I let go, the world around me shimmers and fades.

I grasp the stone once more and all the colors come searing back. The nighttime crickets are growing louder around me. Interesting. So it is my touch—I wasn't just imagining that. I start to release the stone again, though it throbs with regret inside me to even think about letting go. But I have to be sure. I have to be in control.

With a heavy sigh, I release the stone.

❖

I'm back in our room in Mr. Onagi's *ryokan*. The weak evening light is just starting to fade; on the western wall of rice paper, the sunset leaves a harsh orange glow. As if hardly any time at all has passed since I first gripped the stone.

I check the clock on my phone. Correction. *No* time has passed.

Shit. This is worse than being stuck in my life as Reiko: having to live each day twice. I guess I assumed time would skip ahead—like I had been asleep. But it looks like the stone pauses my life here while it pulls me back into the past. As long as I'm making physical contact with it, it seems, then I'm tossed back into Miyu. But the moment I let go, my life here resumes.

I'll leave Miyu alone for now. I have work here to do. I need to find some way to help her escape from her father's arrangement with Tsurube. Maybe if I learn what the shogun are planning—there might be information about it at the historical museum—then I can ensure her father's plans succeed. Then I could barter with him for my freedom.

For Miyu's freedom, I mean.

Fuck. I'm getting way too caught up in this other life. I need a benzo, but I just flushed them all down the toilet. They're probably somewhere out in the East Sea now, making some asshole fish very happy. Or very dead.

I slump back down on the pallet. My gaze skids over the stone. All I want is to go back. But I need to gather information first.

Akiko and Mariko stomp into the room, interrupting my thoughts. "Oh! Hey, Reiko!" Mariko smiles sweetly, so sweetly it stings, when she notices me still awake. "Are you feeling any better? Do you want to come to the club with us tonight?"

"It's been a long day," I reply. "I think I'll get some rest."

The girls turn away from me and start dressing to go out, talking in hushed Japanese. "She's so boring. Look at her, just lying there like a skeleton." At first I think it's Akiko saying it, but then I recognize the shy tone. Mariko. She sounds completely different in Japanese. More bitter, vengeful.

"At least she knows to watch her figure," Aki snaps.

Mariko swallows hard. "I hope your parents are right. That she does kill herself."

Part of me wants to snatch her by the neck, right here and now, and rip her throat open with my bare hands. But I look from her face to Aki's; she's completely desperate to gain Aki's approval no matter what evilness she has to do to get it. Maybe she's not cruel by nature, but so weak she'll do it for Aki's love. She's not even worth the effort it would take me to wrench the life from her.

"Get some rest," Mariko says as they head for the door.

Aki nods. "We have an early morning meeting with the festival coordinator tomorrow." When I stare blankly, she says, "To walk through the festival performance."

"Right," I say. "Sure. Have fun . . ." I force a bitter smile to my face.

As they leave, a flicker of movement catches my eye in the corner by my pallet. It's that goddamned roach again. It hunkers down against the seam between the wall and the mat flooring, hoping, I guess, that I won't notice it.

I slowly turn back my blankets and quietly reach down to grab my slipper from the side of my pallet. No sudden motion. Slipper in hand, I raise my arm above my head. Aim. The roach's antennae twitch. I toss the slipper.

Crunch. The slipper bounces up and down as the roach writhes beneath it. Not dead yet, then, but I've wounded it. I charge across the floor and bring the slipper up, watch the roach hobble along, some of its legs snapped, then bring the slipper down on it again. Forcefully this time.

Then again.

Then again.

It's Akiko. It's Mariko. Goemon and Yodo and my father and the children in the square. Hideki and Chloe and Chloe's new girlfriend, face glistening with red. The deacon at Saint Isaac's. My own real parents, the faceless shadows chained to their startup open–floor plan desks. I smash all of them, watch their guts squish out all over the mats.

I lean back, sitting on my heels, and look at the thick, yellowish goop the roach has turned into.

Then I cross the room and open the mini fridge to dig out Mariko's bag of *onigiri*. She still has three of them tucked away in here. The soft, sticky rice splits open so easily. The roach's guts spread across the middle, no problem. I press the rice balls back together, and they're perfectly formed, the alteration undetectable. I wrap the plastic sheaths of seaweed back around each ball and reassemble the bag.

It's Mariko's punishment for being such a coward, such a glutton, such a traitor to me when she pretends to be my friend.

❖

I dream of the cultural festival. I'm standing on a dais, surrounded by the crowd, as drums beat all around me. As the revelers twirl and clap, something thuds rhythmically, ba-bump, ba-bump, a heart pumping overtime. I stand before the altar and slam the massive mallet into the gong.

Blood gushes from the gong, dripping down the rim of the metal, pouring forth, flooding over the dais steps. Everyone cheers. The drums pick up. The blood flows around my ankles, sticky against my bare flesh.

At the back of the crowd, the fog is coming. It is a thick and tangible thing. It swallows up the crowd, mingles with the blood, roars as it gobbles up more and more. It is coming for me.

I am ready. We are hatred. We are death.

CHAPTER ELEVEN

"WE SAW YOUR FRIEND SIERRA AT THE CLUB LAST night," Mariko says over breakfast, looking right at me. "You should have come with us, Rei-Rei."

She's back in her usual syrupy, shy form, but I know better. I know now how she speaks about me when I shouldn't be able to understand. I refuse to look up as I dish out another heap of rice onto my plate.

God, but I'm starving. These teensy cups of sweet egg and tiny slivers of fish aren't nearly enough to sustain me. I've been starving for weeks. I shovel another chopstick's worth of rice into my mouth. I've forgotten what it's like to want to eat.

"Who's Sierra?" Kazuo asks, without looking up from his Vita. He and Aki are sitting side by side today; they seem to be hoping the table will conceal the fact that her hand is coiled around his thigh.

Kenji glances at me for a moment before answering. "The American girl who works the front desk here in the evenings. I believe she said she teaches English in the next town over."

"Is she hot?" Kazuo asks, in Japanese.

Kenji coughs. "I don't think she's interested in someone like you," he replies, again thinking I can't understand.

"Why? Because she's . . . ?" Kazuo snorts. "I'm sure I can show her the error of her ways."

Mariko and Aki both laugh, though I can't tell if they're laughing with Kazuo or at him. Anger builds inside me, the usual prelude to eruption, but this time I don't want to let it out. Let him be a gross pig. I will take it and take it, like Miyu took it from Goemon. But I will save it, and eventually, I will use it against him, and then the debt will be paid. And it will be a glorious sight.

Maybe Miyu's revenge can help me in my life here, too. She's focused in her hatred. She's in total control. If I can master my plans as Miyu, then I can master my plans as Reiko, too. And I can make everyone pay.

"You're disgusting," Kenji says, but the sound of Tadashi entering covers up his words.

"Hey, losers!" Tadashi calls as he enters the breakfast room. Aki shoots up straight, hand flying out of Kazuo's lap, then stands and flings her arms around Tadashi's neck. He shoves her off. "C'mon, baby, I gotta be able to breathe. Listen up." He pulls his phone from his back pocket. "Opportunity of a lifetime. I just landed Akiko a big interview."

Aki squeals—really, truly squeals—and throws herself around Tadashi again. "You're the best! Oh my God, oh my God! Who's it with?"

"Good grief. Come on, get off me!" Tadashi shoves her off and tugs at his loud floral print shirt to straighten it. "Her name's Morita Suzuki, some shit called 'Special World with Suzuki.'"

"No." Aki clutches one hand to her chest. "No. *Suzuki's Special World?* Are you serious? She has over 300,000 subscribers on YouTube!"

Tadashi's blank expression gives him away—he's never heard of her—but he quickly recovers with a sly grin. "Only the best for my girl."

Maybe I shouldn't have eaten that second helping of rice. I have the sudden urge to hurl.

Tadashi turns to address the rest of us. "All right, losers, we need aki * LIFE * rhythm to be flawless today, got it? We've got one hour to set up for the interview. Start teasing the interview on social media. Record a few clips for the site, get some shots of the crowd. Remind everyone about the festival, and hint that we're dropping something *big* real soon. *Big time.* We are big time. This is our big opportunity." He claps twice. "Now act it."

Our big opportunity. Aki's, he means. God, but I'd love to see her fall on her face. I could wreck her interview with Suzuki, but something tells me it'll only be the stepping-stone. *Suzuki's Special World* will turn the hyperconnected J-pop eye Aki's way. That's when I need to be ready.

But first, I need to find out more information for Miyu. Maybe after Aki's interview, I can slip off to the historical museum. I follow the others, antsy, out the door.

Kuramagi is awash in tourists. The streets look more alive, more like they do when I'm inhabiting Miyu, but with an extra heaping of tackiness ladled on top like watery gravy. A busload of retirees disgorges wave after wave of elderly Japanese with walkers and parasols and canes. Every souvenir shop and *yakitori* skewer stand has a slime trail of tourists queuing up outside, waiting their turn to pay for their over-priced handmade bowls and dolls. Parents make halfhearted attempts to usher their children, whose mouths are smeared black and purple from the charcoal ice-cream cups.

Then we reach the village square, where work crews are setting up all of the stages and side tents for the cultural festival. My breath hitches in my throat like I've swallowed something down the wrong way. It looks exactly like the dais in my dream last night. I clench my fists at my sides as a wave of anger rolls over me. I'm just *livid*, but I don't even know what I'm angry about. I want to see blood pouring down that stage, feel the bones of someone's head condense and crunch between my hands—

Jesus. What the hell is wrong with me? Have I always been this violent? When Chloe put the red-dipped paintbrush in my hand, the violence was only an expression. An allegory. I didn't actually want to hurt anyone back then—at least, I don't think I did. *Yeah, Reiko. You keep telling yourself that.* That's what I told the therapists, after all. It's what I told our small groups in the ward. I left out the part about my scars, though I knew the orderlies already knew. I don't want to hurt anyone.

But I do want to make them pay. Feel them squash like the roach beneath my shoe. Show them who has the last laugh. Make them pay for the hurt *they've* done.

"How about this platform over here for taking photographs?" Kenji calls, climbing up onto a viewing platform. It connects to the balcony of one of the nicer houses on the edge of the village square, the elaborate finials at the roof joints glint in the weak sun.

Aki props her fists on her hips and squints up at the stand, no doubt trying to frame herself in the shot in her mind. "Okay. Rei, get up there and see what you can do for lighting."

I climb up onto the platform, swaying momentarily as a breeze rattles the plywood, but regain my balance. Kenji's looking at me suspiciously, so I give him a hearty scowl and pull out my handheld camcorder. The lighting's terrible today—overcast, with thicker clouds darkening the shadows at irregular intervals—but it's the best we're going to get.

"Okay. If you keep your back to this mountain, it should look good while still giving the right color balance."

Aki gives me a wink and a smooch, and Mariko climbs up to give her a final powdering.

"Go easy on the bronzer," Aki tells her in Japanese. "Suzuki always cakes it on way too thick, and I want to make sure I look soft and refreshing compared to her."

"Not a problem. I'll stash it away for our later . . . plan."

Then they very definitely both look at me.

Um. What the hell are they planning? What does it have to do with me? And bronzer? I'm almost tempted to give away my secret, that I understand them now, but there would be too many questions I'm not ready to answer. Too many things to explain.

"Okay!" Aki forces a wide grin on her face and adjusts her cropped shirt. She's going for a fresh-faced, wholesome girl-next-door kind of look today. I'm not sure how that's supposed to sell aki * LIFE * rhythm to Suzuki's fans, but who cares what I think? "Reiko, get ready to roll."

I flip the camcorder open, give her a bored countdown, and hit Record.

"Hello, my beautiful aki * LIFE * rhythm lifestylists! It is such a deep honor to be reaching you today from the village of Kuramagi, in Gifu Prefecture! You may wonder what such an old-fashioned place like Kuramagi has to do with our life rhythm, but you'd be surprised—there's plenty we can learn about our future by weaving in bits of the past!"

It's all I can do not to drop the camcorder in disgust. Her stupid videos are even worse now that I know what she's actually saying.

"I've curated quite the collection of unusual Aki pieces for you already, and I'll be featuring them here in a little bit. But first, I'm so excited to announce that later this evening, you can find me on Morita Suzuki's channel. The address is right . . . here!" She points to the empty air beside her, where we'll add a link button in post-production. I can already hear the twinkling sound effect that will accompany the button's appearance. "That's all for now. Keep your heart pure and your eyes open, and enjoy . . . aki . . . life . . . *rhythm*."

I flip the camcorder shut.

"Great work, babe, great work." Tadashi is applauding behind me. "Suzuki'll be here soon, so make sure you've got everything the way you want it."

"Am I done?" I ask, in terse English. Between the uneven light, Aki's saccharine performance, and my enormous—in relative terms—breakfast, I'm feeling pretty queasy. Like something's trying to take root right in my gut.

"Are you kidding? I need you to get behind-the-scenes

photos." Aki jabs one finger at me. "This is *Morita Suzuki*. Of the *Suzuki's Special World* channel. I need documentation. Bonus features for subscribers."

I grimace and stuff the camcorder back into the bag. Kenji waves me over to the tiered roof of the building, where he crouches, sketching Aki. "What the hell is so special about this Suzuki, anyway?" I ask, as I climb up beside him.

"Well, let's see. She lives in a beautiful apartment in Akakusa, funded entirely by revenue from her YouTube channel . . . Hmmm . . . She used to be in an *aidoru* band, but that actually came about from her internet fame, and not the other way around like it usually does."

Aidoru—the manufactured pop groups that are as much about marketing their members, or *aidoru* (idols) as the weapons-grade pop music. Just one portion of the market aki * LIFE * rhythm is seeking to infiltrate. "And why is she bothering with someone like Aki?"

Kenji shrugs. "Probably because she used to sleep with Tadashi."

"No. Wait. Seriously?" I laugh. "Tadashi?"

"You realize he used to be a big name, don't you?" Kenji asks. "It was a long time ago, but you can probably still find schoolgirls with his poster taped up in their rooms."

"Ew. No." I wrinkle my nose. "I thought his money was from his dad, or something . . ."

"Oh, it is. He burned through his *aidoru* money a long

time ago, trying and failing to be a big-shot manager. Now look where that landed him."

"Right in our pathetic midst." The cosmic justice feels delicious.

"What's the matter?" Kenji asks, squinting at me with that wry grin on his lips. "Tadashi isn't exactly your idea of an Asian heartthrob?"

"Gross. Definitely not." I tuck my knees under my chin. "I don't go for the big meathead guys."

Kenji is quiet for a few moments. "But you do, um . . ." Then he brushes his hair down over his forehead. "Never mind."

"What?" I ask. My stomach tightens around too many servings of rice.

He darkens the line of Aki's chin on his drawing. "You do go for . . ." He winces. "Guys."

I stare at him.

"It's okay if not. It's just—" His shoulders draw forward as he curls around his drawing. "I saw how you and Sierra talk, back at the inn, and I thought maybe . . ."

The tightness inside of me is imploding, crushing down hard, turning into a diamond of hatred. "Is that a problem if I'm bisexual?" I ask. "So what if I like boys and girls? What if I don't like anyone at all?" The darkness flashes through me—the rivers and rivers of blood. I raise my hand in front of me and imagine it drenched in red. It feels sticky, throbbing, *alive*. Yes, this is what I'm after. This is what I—

No, Reiko.

God. No. Now I'm truly losing it. Why the hell did I get rid of my meds?

Oh, right. Because I thought they were making me crazy. Now how's *that* for cosmic justice?

"Well," Kenji says, "then I think that's your right. And if you don't want to tell me, that's your right, too." He flips his pencil over to erase. "I only thought I'd ask."

I roll back onto the roof and stare up at the splotchy sky, the mountains that erode into the clouds across the valley from us. "How much time do you have?"

Kenji looks down at the interview, just getting under way, and gives me a look.

"Fine." I close my eyes. "There was this girl at summer arts camp. Chloe. And she . . . possessed me."

She'd done far more than possess me. She had crawled under my flesh and taken control of me. I danced to her tune; I moved on her strings. And the worst of it was that I believed she'd set me free.

"She told me I could be more," I said.

Oh, she'd said, looking at my camp application portfolio. She'd cooed the word like she was reviewing a toddler's first stab at art. *Look how cute you were. Your gossamer-winged fairies and shit.*

I'd snatched the portfolio back from her. It was a collage featuring my elven sorceress from Legends of Eldritch Journey;

I'd pasted the deep, gray-throated blue of the Sound into the shape of her hair, and stitched her dress together from my photographs at the botanical guardians. *She's . . . she's an elf,* I'd muttered. *Not a fairy.*

"I wanted to impress her. Prove to her that I could be a serious artist. That I could be a serious person." I swallow. "Be hers."

I'd flipped through the folio until I found the piece I was looking for—the one I knew was serious enough, meaningful enough, *art* enough to impress her. All her art was meant to accomplish something, to tear down the patriarchy or chastise the oppressor class. She stood for something. She cared. Back then, I wanted to care, too. *Here, this—this is my favorite. A meditation on . . .* What would catch her attention? Prove to her I understood things? *War.*

It was a montage of Hideki photographs, meandering across a sand-strewn canvas. Hideki, the boy who ran off to the desert so he wouldn't have to rely on our parents to pay for med school. I'd assembled it from photos he sent back from the front. Grainy webcam snaps of him in the computer room with exhaustion plump and oily under his eyes. Hideki in his scrubs, probably smiling beneath that surgeon's mask, not that it ever reached his eyes. In the bed of a truck, the photographer (handsome, shirtless, I noticed) reflected in his sunglasses. Snippets pulled from his official discharge.

They only told half the story. My canvas of bodies and wounds and nude figures told the rest.

One, two, three, four, five. I'd pressed the bruises while I waited for Chloe to approve.

Her gaze lingered on the rivers of red that fed the canvas's desert. *Yes.* Her fingers traced them. I wondered how she would look, sticky with blood. *I knew there was a revolution in you.*

Upheaval. I wanted my own upheaval. I wanted to become what Chloe believed me to be.

"I call it. *Don't Tell,*" I'd said, and pointed to the bits of gauze I'd taped over Hideki's bruised mouth. The photo his prosecutor used as proof against the defendants, to secure Hideki the lightning-fast honorable discharge and his quick ticket back to the States. The portfolio photograph didn't quite capture the effort I'd made to soak the gauze in red paint, to arrange it just so on the canvas. But I think she got the idea.

Chloe's smile spread wide. *Art gives us the power to change.*

I wanted to change myself. Into whatever she wanted me to be. Anything to be loved. To be needed. Then I would have the power. Then I could possess her, too.

"But it wasn't meant to last," I say. "She had chaos in her veins. Restlessness. She was always seeking. She went back home after camp, and that's when I lost her."

I leave out the part about my violent photographs, the ones she hired someone to hang up at the school. And the night that came before, cold and rainy, watching Chloe and her new girlfriend, hand in hand. The shattered glass that glittered like raindrops on the street. My hands. Trembling.

"You aren't alone," Kenji whispers.

I fight back a laugh. I'm always alone.

"I had a girlfriend all through high school. Our parents wanted us to marry. She was best friends with this other guy, Hiro—everyone knew he was gay. So I never worried about her spending time with him. He'd go shopping with her, hang out at the cat cafés, all the things my friends would laugh at me for doing. I didn't do those things because they would say that I was gay, too."

I feel the restless twitch in my legs that I used to get during small groups in the psych ward. A weariness with all these people, all their tales. All their stupid problems, sucking like lampreys at their brains. I fight the twitching down. I don't hate Kenji, not in the same way I hate all the rest. At least, I don't hate him yet.

"But I resented that I wasn't getting to share a part of her life, you know? So I made an effort to spend time with them both. At first, it was awkward; I didn't think Hiro and I had much in common aside from her. He didn't care about comics, anything like that. But then something . . . changed."

I turn my head toward him.

"He was kind, when he wasn't putting on a show for people. Encouraged my art. When my girlfriend insisted I go to university and get a good salaryman job, he suggested I focus more on what *I* wanted to do. And then, the better I got to know him, learned all the things he longed to do with his life . . ." Kenji trails off, his cheeks burning deep crimson.

"Oh, no. You and Hiro had a fling, didn't you?" I laugh when he doesn't deny it. "Wow. Falling for your girlfriend's boyfriend. Straight out of a *shonen-ai* manga."

Kenji peers at me from the corner of his eye. "It wasn't cheating—not like it means in English. It was never that physical, and she—she knew about us. Thought it was cute, you know, like the Boy Love comics she read. It didn't change how I felt about her, except that I felt weird, being pulled between two people . . . And then I started to see the jealousy in each of them. They weren't best friends anymore. They weren't even on speaking terms."

"So I ended it. With both of them."

I let out a low whistle. "What did your parents say?"

"Well, this was around the same time I decided not to go to university, so . . . let's just say they had plenty to yell at me about those days."

"Hey! Quiet on the set!" Tadashi shouts up to us, from the platform. I roll back up to sitting and nearly fall over. Suzuki's hair is styled in a hot pink bouffant, and she's wearing skin-tight baby blue vinyl pants. The streaky aftereffects of spray-on tanner mar her arms and her exposed belly button. Actual full-sized action figures—they look like some sort of mech suit from one anime or another—swing from both of Suzuki's ears. Special World, indeed. I'm starting to see what Aki meant about not even wanting to try competing with all of *that*.

I pull out my snapshot camera and grab a few quick shots— the texture of Suzuki's hair, the way she has to peel the curls out of her makeup in the wind—then crawl down to the edge of the roof to frame her with Aki at her side. I manage to catch a good shot of Aki and Suzuki both laughing, looking about as genuine as I imagine either of them is capable of being. Aki glances at me, questioning; I give her a thumbs up, then crawl back up the roofline to join Kenji again.

"You're like a regular Peter Parker with that camera," Kenji says. "Nice acrobatics."

Aki's trembling as Suzuki's cameraman gets ready to record. God, this stupid little staged chat means so much to her. And then this whole big production. The festival performance, and the meager *aidoru* media attention she hopes it will draw.

At first, I thought I could use the performance to humiliate her. I could sabotage her costume, for instance. An epic wardrobe malfunction would be just the thing to get her plenty of press, and none of it the kind she wants. I could rig a light to fall on stage, or set up the microphone to shock her.

But it all sounds so tame to me now. Like a childish prank. I need something grander. Something more powerful.

The buzzing rises in the back of my mind. *Violence,* I find myself thinking. *Upheaval. Renewal.*

Okay, Reiko, you've got to get it together. Don't be the monster Chloe made everyone think you are.

But what if I am? What if I'm so much more?

Suddenly I'm on the red-stained dais again. All eyes are on me as the blood drips from my slit throat. All eyes are on the blood, bathing my arms, pumping from my veins. So much blood. It can't all be mine. Fog snaring my ankles and wrists, devouring everything in its path—

"Hey. Are you okay?" Kenji touches my arm, gentle.

"I'm fine," I snarl, which I realize doesn't exactly make my point.

He pulls his arm back. "You just . . . had that look."

"For fuck's sake, Kenji." I curl my arms around my legs. "Stop trying to be my goddamned nanny."

He lowers his pencil; his face looks so soft, like if I punched it, my fist would just sink in. God, I want to punch him. I want to punch everyone. "Can I just try to be your friend?" he asks.

Friends. Right. Everyone wants to be friends with the antisocial whackjob. Because I'm such a caring and thoughtful friend. Because I'm so charismatic and charming. "I'm not a good person, Kenji," I tell him. When I blink, I still see the bloody trails. I still hear the roaring buzz. And I crave the feel of hot red on my hands.

Kenji lets his breath out slowly. "There's a difference between doing something bad, and being bad."

"No. No, you don't understand." I tug at the leather bracelets on my right wrist. One, two, three, four, five. "There's something . . . inside of me." I squeeze the five bruises hard. Can't let them fade. "A rotten core."

I don't know how I expected him to react, but he only watches me, as calm as if he were waiting for his tea to steep. "Why do you think that?" he finally asks.

I squeeze harder. The pain spirals through me, painting fractals on the backs of my eyelids. Everything is framed in black, like I'm trying to watch the world through a pinhole. I have to tear it wide.

"I want to do bad things," I hear myself say, fuzzy and distant. "To others. To myself."

I thought Chloe was wrong about me. I thought they all were wrong. That I didn't really want to do those things I painted in the collage. But this is more than vengeance. This is a primal need. To hurt, and be hurt. That rottenness inside me is stronger than ever before.

I want—need—to make everyone pay. Let them see my hurt laid bare. My final masterpiece, wrought from my need from vengeance. It burns inside me. It's what Miyu would do. And I want to do it, too.

Suddenly, I know how.

"Reiko . . ." Kenji looks at me like I'm something fragile, something he shouldn't expose to direct light. It makes me hate him. "Why did you come here?" he asks. "To Japan. I mean—" He shakes his head. "I'm glad you're here, but I don't know why you thought it would solve your problems."

"You think I'm trying to solve them?" The laugh that rises out of me is harsh; it scrapes against my throat. "It doesn't matter where I go. It only makes everything worse."

"What are you afraid of?" he asks. "What are you running from?"

"I don't know, okay? I only know that—" And then it hits me, right in the chest, powerful as a boulder. "This is where I'm meant to be."

Yes. This is where I'm meant to be—this valley, this festival, this confluence of time and space. The perfect setting for my last revenge. I can almost feel the comforting chill of the black stone in my camera bag. This is the place. This is where it all has to happen.

I'm going to help Miyu. And then I'm going to bring the whole festival down.

CHAPTER TWELVE

I THOUGHT AKI'S INTERVIEW WITH SUZUKI WENT just fine, but she's in rare form the whole way back to the inn. "Let me see the photos you took, Reiko." She tries to yank my camera bag straight out of my hand. "I can't trust Suzuki's team to pick the ones that flatter *me* most. They're going to pick the ones that look best for her."

I yank my camera bag right back. Anger crawls up the back of my neck, prickling the wispy hairs there. "They turned out perfect, as always. Leave me alone. And don't you dare touch my bag again."

Aki stops dead in her tracks, appalled that I could even think to defy her. "Excuse me?"

The heat of anger spreads like a rash. It gives me power

and strength. Soon enough, this will all be over. And everyone will be sorry. "I said to leave me alone."

The late autumn chatter of birds swells around us, thick as a fog. Tadashi, Kazuo, and Mariko all seem to take a step back. As if the world is nothing but me and Akiko, and this heavy, roaring quiet.

Then Akiko shrugs and plunges down the *ryokan*'s main path.

My anger keeps buzzing, tearing through me, swelling all around. I have to let it out. Normally I would cut, but this time I think I need another sensation. I need Miyu. I need to slip back into her life, live as someone else, escape from this panic and rage. It's safe for me this way, I tell myself. A healthy outlet. I can spend just a little more time in Miyu's life, learn a bit more, and then I can gather the information I need to help her. I can muster up the will to do what needs to be done in my own life.

Mr. Onagi's face is as deep red as his bean paste when we return to the inn. He swoops from behind the counter and plants himself right in Akiko's path.

"I know what you've been doing," he says with deathly calm, his Japanese as ragged as a saw. "I know you've been sneaking out of my inn after curfew."

Akiko blinks a couple times. "Huh?"

"You don't understand, do you? The rules are there for a reason. Rules are meant to be *obeyed*." Fear coats his words. "I can't let you threaten the safety of my inn. "I'll throw you out. I have no moral obligation to keep you here. If you can't follow one simple rule—"

"Would you relax?" she snaps right back. "It's not a big deal. This town is so dull, and your inn is so dull. Of course we have to go elsewhere for entertainment."

"You have no idea what you're messing with!" Mr. Onagi whispers. "The rule is here for a reason. And it *must* be observed!"

I suddenly remember I'm not supposed to be able to understand what they're saying, so I turn toward Mariko, who's hanging near the inn's entrance with me as I unlace my boots. "What's he so scared about?" I ask.

"Oh . . ." Mariko pauses for a moment, then shrugs. "He's just, uh . . . excited for the show. You know how old guys are. A little batty, right? Is that how you say it?"

"Yeah. Batty," I say through gritted teeth. I slide out of my boots, hop into the red plastic house slippers, and shuffle my way past the altercation to the restrooms and lock myself in a stall. By the time I click the stall shut, I've got the stone buzzing in my hand.

✦

I am hunched down in the kitchens of the *honjin*, arms submerged up to my elbows in sudsy, filthy water. I stagger

backward, nearly losing my balance, finding myself mani-
fested in Miyu's body in the midst of her doing something
else. The thought makes my stomach churn—Miyu living
her life, proceeding along, *existing*, without my involvement.
My life in the present pauses while I'm with Miyu. But
whatever happens here seems to exist in some hidden pocket
of time.

Miyu is a real person, with a life all her own. Well—
obviously. But where does she go when I inhabit her? Is she still
within this body, controlling the memories I can access? Or,
maybe she didn't know about me? The possibility gives me a
thrill. A stolen joyride in someone else's life. Does she remember the time I spend in her body, even if only in a fog? Or does
it leave her grasping for clues, just like the rest of her life left me?

I know that feeling of falling asleep in my own life, when
my conscious thought shuts down and muscle memory takes
control. Sometimes, I jerk awake in the middle of driving, or
walking a familiar path, and can't remember the thoughts
and acts that led me there. That's how it feels when I am
Miyu, and I find her body carrying out processes that my
mind has never learned. Like that moment of jerking awake.
But being in Miyu's body is the real awakening; it makes my
life as Reiko feel like a blur. And I want to be awake, to stay
alive as Miyu. Her hate burns so clear, while my own is a
murky flicker. If I could become Miyu, then Reiko could
doze forever.

"Quit daydreaming," says a sharp voice behind me. Yodo. "Those dishes won't scrub themselves."

I rock forward again and dive my hands into the washbasin. "Sorry," I mutter, and resume Miyu's work. Weak daylight, the color of runny eggs, dribbles across the kitchen; I was probably scrubbing away the remains of the samurais' breakfast. Unbidden, I feel a pang at the thought of having missed out on a chance to talk to Jiro. I grip the rag tighter as I scrub away his leftovers. I wonder if he recited any more poetry to me or if he commented on our conversation from last night. I wonder if Miyu reacted to him the same way that I did, or if she was confused by their new camaraderie.

Then I remember Goemon's awful reptilian stare, and I'm glad not to have seen it again.

Yodo is beating something behind me like it owes her money; the smell tells me it is rice balls she is turning into *mochi*. "I see the way you chatter with that junior samurai," she says, in between vicious thwacks. "Don't forget yourself. That your father promised you to Tsurube."

My shoulders tense. Who is this Tsurube who thinks he can lay some sort of claim to my life? "Nothing wrong with being kind to our guests," I say, though for all I know, it violates some vital Confucian principle. The ones my father has supposedly beat into me, although I can't remember them. The dishes rattle in the basin.

"Careful! Don't break those dishes," she hisses, then

returns to the beating. "Such a clumsy fool, for someone who thinks herself a great seductress. You could have done us all a favor and run off to the Gion District in Kyoto. Beg some whorehouse to take you in. I suppose you think a *hatamoto* will offer you a better life than Tsurube? You're even more foolish than you look."

I stop. In the basin, my fist closes around the hilt of a filleting knife. The bone handle fits just right in the fold of my palm. I take a deep breath and let it out. "Why are you so cruel to me?" I ask. "What do you care what becomes of me?"

Yodo isn't my mother—I am certain of that much. She is too awkward around my father and too boastful around me. I don't have any definite memories of her, but I have a sense she's worked for Miyu's family for some time. A widow, maybe, looking to make ends meet now that she doesn't have a husband to care for her. Isn't that what Jiro said? Women have no property, no independence in this age. Maybe her own insecurity in her lot led her to lash out at me.

But as she laughs, I can tell she feels certain I am the one at fault.

"You think you are blameless? A senseless victim? Don't be absurd. Go ask your mother why I hate you. Better yet— your sister, too." She scoffs. "You're nothing but a gutter snipe. A useless scrap of fabric, the wrong size and shape to stitch into anything good."

Sister. My breath falters. The lopsided emptiness of Miyu's

bedroom. Of course she had a sister—it all makes sense. The room was built for two girls; without the sister's things in it, it looks all wrong. Two girls, just like the wall scroll depicts. But what happened to her?

What did Miyu do to her? With a feeling like a puncture wound, I probe Miyu's mind but my memories offer up nothing. Maybe Miyu can sense me, feel me taking over her body and mind, and refuses to share her secrets with me.

Fine. She can keep her secrets. I have other plans.

Once I finish with the dishes for Yodo, she leaves to tidy up the rest of the *honjin*, and Father finds me before I have a chance to track down something else to occupy myself with. "Miyu. Quietly. Listen to me." He grips me by the shoulders with his thick bear paws. "I need you to handle some errands for me. It's absolutely vital that you do them properly."

Good lord, what is everyone's problem with me? I've driven off my sister somehow, I understand that much now, but I've yet to see any hard proof of Miyu's incompetence that vexes everyone so much. "Of course, Father. What do you need?"

His grip tightens; it feels like talons digging in. It reminds me, with a dull ache, of Hideki. Then he releases me with a curt nod. "Head to the town center. You need to purchase sake from the brewer there—but I want you to pay careful attention to the village square and how it's being decorated for the festival. I need to know everything. The layout of the structures, where the town guards are positioned, whether any of the shogun's forces have arrived yet."

Father needs information about something he doesn't want the samurai to know.

"*Hai*, Father. I'll give you a full account." What does it matter to me? I have no stake in politics, in the constant tug of war between the nobility and the military. From what Jiro said the night before, neither does he, beyond the bare minimum of duties he is obligated to observe by his rank. I'll observe and report, and who cares what Father and his friends do with the information.

"Everything, Miyu." His stare fixes me through like a sword pinning me in place. "I need you to remember everything. But don't let anyone notice what you're doing."

Miyu may disappoint these people when I'm not around, but she'll live up to them on my watch. I thrust my shoulders back and meet his stare. "I won't forget."

I slip into my *geta* and wind my way toward the village square, an eerie sense of déjà vu falling like a shadow over me. I can't help but notice all the ways this Kuramagi compares and contrasts with my own world's version—the buildings fresh with still-green wood and new paint, and delicate hand-stitched banners and lanterns, but also the dim, grimy shops that bear no electric lights or modern food storage techniques. I have to give the people credit, though, for their attention to cleanliness; even without modern water heaters and indoor plumbing, they smell better than your average Seattle hippie.

But there sure are a lot of them. A teeming salmon spawn of humanity, crawling over each other as they go about their business preparing for the festival, from the venerated farmers hauling in rice and Asian cabbage and persimmons to the lowly merchants hawking their wares on every street corner and beneath every awning. And once again, all the people— no matter their age, their rank, the number of children in tow—part around me like I am a cold no one can afford to catch. I am untouchable. I am diseased.

For once, it doesn't bother me.

I feel powerful. Like some kind of vengeful goddess. It makes me feel alive to see their stares, their fear, their wide-eyed whispering.

It makes me want to be alive.

In the distance, the drummers practice for the coming festivities: first the festival performance, then the purification ceremony. I imagine the thudding of my heart falling in sync with them, of each hammer fall striking like a blow. I am Reiko and I am Miyu and I am powerful, and no one can ever make me feel tiny again.

Finally I reach the village square, where dozens of workers are assembling the platforms and makeshift shrines. Buddhist monks and Shinto priests work side by side to issue blessings on the new construction, warding them from malicious spirits and from the earthly yearnings of man. I make a mental map of the area, like I used to make in my head when preparing a photo shoot—noting all the objects in the space, the way the light falls on them, the risks they pose in sticking out from behind people's heads or casting a strange shadow.

Then I spot the soldiers.

Jiro and Goemon are huddled with one man, wearing the plated armor of a *bakufu* officer. Behind him, an uneasy collection of soldiers in less elaborate garb scan the crowd. I follow their line of sight; one of the builders, I notice, isn't actually doing any assembly, but instead is watching the crowd and occasionally looking back to the soldiers with a subtle nod. Another merchant, curiously uninterested in shouting down the other peddlers in the square, behaves similarly.

So the shogun's servants haven't come here to review some stupid records at the feudal lord's castle. They are here to monitor us.

To monitor my father, perhaps—and whatever it is he and his friends mean to do.

I study the soldiers' faces, quickly, trying to keep my face angled away so Jiro and Goemon won't recognize me and the others won't catch me staring. I make a note of the man whose face droops like a horse and the broad-bellied man with the dangerous hawk eyes. Then I hurry on to the brewer's shop.

"Miyu, Miyu, Mad Miyu," a little girl chants, maybe four or five years old, darting across my path. Her soft slippers make a whispering echo as she runs—*mi-yu-mi-yu-mi-yu*.

"Watch yourself," I mutter at her, but she's already disappeared back into the throng. I shake my head and raise my chin high. Miyu is powerful, confident—there's no disguising her hate or hiding it away in her thoughts. As Miyu, I let it boil over. I am a goddess of vengeance. No one can threaten me. Certainly not a little child.

The brewer takes one look at me, plops a wire rack of four sake bottles on the counter, and taps two fingers against the surface. Apparently not everyone wants to taunt me endlessly. Some would rather have nothing to do with me at all. I grab a fistful of coins from my pocket, fingers brushing up against the heavy black stone. It feels hot, like I left it out to bake in the sun. The warmth strengthens me.

As soon as the brewer has counted out the coins—twice—he nods and shoos me away.

Great. Thanks *so* much. I grip the wooden handle and hoist the rack off the counter, muscles pinching as I lift. I'm not used to carrying anything much heavier than my camera bag these days. But I remind myself I've carried around way more than this, back before everything—that I am stronger than I know.

I head back into the square. Brightly colored rectangles of

fabric flap in the wind where they've been strung up around the periphery. "Miyu, Miyu, mad Miyu!" This time a little boy goes whizzing past me, right in my path, nearly making me trip over the hem of my own stupid kimono. I catch myself, slide back into my wooden sandals, and grit my teeth.

Laughter rings out behind me, then melts into the background noise. Through the corner of my eye, I scout for Jiro and Goemon again, but they aren't in my periphery.

"Miyu, mad Miyu!" a chorus of children's voices shout, from behind me.

I swivel on one foot. "Okay, seriously now—"

Splat.

Hot, oozing stink runs down the side of my face and coils around my throat. I stagger backward, the sake carrier slipping from my hand. Red and brown blur my vision. The warm goo soaks through my skin and slithers through my hair. With shaking hands, I paw at the—the *thing* that now slides down the side of my face and onto my shoulder.

My hand comes away slick with blood, and my fingers tangle with pink, lumpy tubes.

Oh, God. Miyu's breakfast lurches up toward my throat as the stench overwhelms me. Some sort of animal's organs—intestines, blood, slop all tangled together. I peel it off my shoulder and scrub the blood from my face. Yet I am outside of myself, calm, focused, determined. I am Miyu now. I know precisely how to handle this.

Scrub it away from me.

Find the kids who did this.

And rip their own goddamned organs out to see how they like wearing them draped around their necks.

The drumbeats from the square build and build under my skin; the red marring my vision comes from inside of me now. The maniacal laughter around me—children and adults alike—pinches with an anxiousness, then fades completely. I clench one hand into a fist, and spin, looking for the closest target to strike—

"Miyu." Suddenly someone is cupping their arm around my other shoulder and steering me away from the small crowd that has formed. "Miyu, you're all right."

Jiro's voice. I barely recognize it through my rage. Everything sounds jagged and threatening, a world of sharp corners. I want to shred myself apart.

No, first I will shred everyone else.

"Come on, Miyu. Let's get you cleaned up." Jiro's grip is firm on my elbow as he guides me through the square. He doesn't have to do much; people trip over themselves to get out of our way. "It's fine. You're going to be all right."

"Let her suffer!" someone shouts after us. "Make her suffer like she's done to all of us!"

But no one takes up the invitation to pile on.

I imagine my dream of the town square—the rivers of blood pouring down the dais. The one we pass looks just like the one in my Kuramagi, which also looks like the one in my dream. A need both rabid and frightfully calm rises inside me.

The *honjin* is empty when we return; Yodo is off doing her other odd jobs, and Father is probably conspiring with his friends. Jiro leads me straight to the bathing room and sets the coals aflame around the spare bucket of bathwater.

"Let's get your outer robe off first," he says, gesturing to the *obi*, now slimy with offal, tied around my waist.

My fingers fumble with the complex knots and bows that hold it in place. I am trembling; I feel like I can shudder and shake right out of my skin. I feel like one of the coals, hissing and cracking open, crumbling into ash. I want to catch flame.

"Shh." Jiro cups his hands around mine. "Let me."

Somehow, I manage a weak nod.

Jiro frowns a bit, but finally manages to thread one wide end of the *obi* out of the other, and tugs the belting loose. It crumples to the ground. He opens one flap of the outer kimono, then the other, then eases them both off my shoulders, taking care not to let the soiled exterior touch the undergarment robe beneath, then drapes the kimono over a wooden rack nearby.

"There. Much better already." He smiles at me, but it looks so sad it makes me furious all over again. It is all I can do not to strangle him—strangle anyone foolish enough to get in my reach. I don't want his pity, or anyone else's.

I want revenge.

Jiro dips a towel into the waterbasin while it heats and begins to scrub my face—roughly enough to strip away the crust of viscera that has begun to dry, but not so roughly that he tears my flesh. I sit, silent and seething, while he works. A furrow appears in his brow as he scrubs; his fingers cradle the rag with loving precision. There is something tender in the way he works. A care that I suspect I don't deserve.

"Don't you want to know?" I ask, unable to stand it any longer. "Doesn't it matter to you why everyone hates me so?" I want to know, after all. Surely he does, too. If he knew the darkness in Miyu's heart—in *my* heart—would he run from me? Or draw even nearer?

He scrubs at my temple and into my hairline. "Should it?"

I press my lips into a thin line.

"We are all defined by our past," Jiro says. "Our choices and circumstances have made us who we are. It's all there, carved into us indelibly. But . . . it is not our present. Nor our future. That's what we control. It's what we choose to do with the past that is entirely up to us."

"Well, some people have more options than others." I fold my arms and fight back a fresh surge of tears. My past. Chloe had turned my feelings, a momentary inspired spasm of hatred, into my present and my future. Hideki had always tormented me, and then, when I needed him most, tried to remove himself from my life entirely. Who knows what threads of Miyu's past are forever closed off to her? The past is like the hungry fog of my dreams, forever creeping back over us when we think we are in the clear.

Jiro's fingers brush against my lip; his gaze moves from my skin to my eyes. "You seem like the sort of woman capable of shaping her own future." He holds my gaze with the same steadiness he now uses to cup my chin, with certainty as his fingers feather against my mouth. "Of claiming what you're owed."

My breath hitches in my throat. "If I ever get the chance."

"There're always more chances than we realize." He swallows, audible in the cavernous bathing room. We stare at each other for a moment as the coals crackle and hiss. "We never know when a new opportunity will come exactly where we never expect to find it."

I look at his lips, thin and angled, a soft hue against his lighter flesh. His warm brown eyes beg me to lose myself in them. The gentle curves of his face. He leans toward me, smelling of pine and plums.

"Miyu," he murmurs, like a dark curse. "You strike me as the kind of girl unable to leave debts unpaid. But also not one to leave your desires unfulfilled." His dark eyes glisten. "You're stronger than you know."

Oh, God. I squeeze my eyes shut. Oh, God. I am falling so hard for this long-dead samurai. I am falling so hard for him, and I'm not even myself, I'm not even certain how I am able to be here with him at all.

When I open my eyes, Jiro has leaned back, but with a smile on his face. "I'll, ah . . . I'll let you get cleaned up." He tosses the rag onto the heap of soiled clothing, then goes to dump the heated water into the tub for me. "Call if you need anything more."

The panel slides shut behind him, leaving me alone with the frantic hammering of my heart.

I start to strip off my undergarments, then remember the stone. I need to keep it on me if I want to stay in this century— that's what I have figured out. I glance around for a minute, then settle on the spare sash I wear around my secondary robe. With a few twists, I manage to secure the stone in the sash, then wrap the sash tight around my ankle. I take a few tentative steps across the bamboo mats. The sling holds firm.

Something unfurls in my chest, like a tightly laced garment easing loose. I am safe here. I belong in this world.

I pull the pins out of my hair and shake it loose, then begin to scrub the rest of Miyu's body. My body now. Miyu's body looks so strange to me—soft around the edges, where the former me had vicious jutting bones and stretch marks. The smooth expanse of her stomach and thighs where Reiko's body was lined with perfect scars. Yet Jiro is right. She feels . . . strong. Powerful in a way I never felt as myself. I know she's withstood so much—whatever cruelty caused the villagers of Kuramagi and even her own father to turn on her. Whatever put the rift between her sister and herself.

Sturdy. That was Miyu. Formidable. Strong. Fearsome.

She deserves to be feared and revered. I will make them fear and revere her.

I scrub her flesh until it is pink and renewed; I soak all the blood and bits of viscera from her sleek black hair. I stand in the steamy chamber, raw, feeling reborn.

A loose cotton *yukata* waits for me on a nearby hook; I wrap it around me, left over right, twist my damp hair back up on top of my head, and then leave the washroom.

The panel of Jiro's guestroom is cracked open, inviting. I find him huddled over a small leather notebook, a quill curled in his hand. He glances up at me where I stand, peering through the doorway, and beckons me inside. Tentatively, I poke one bare foot into his room, and then the next.

"There you are. Just as beautiful as always." His smile glows like lamplight. "Are you feeling better now?"

"Much. Thank you." I take another step toward him. "You didn't have to help me. But thank you."

He lowers the quill into his book and closes the journal around it, then sets it aside. "Of course I did."

"And—and thank you for what you said." I am standing close to him, now. I could reach out and wrap my arms around him, press his face against my thighs. He looks so warm and inviting. Soft and enveloping as a freshly made bed. My fingers twitch where I'd hooked them around my belt, and I see his muscles tighten, his slight inhale.

"I, uh . . ." He swallows and peels his gaze from me. "I meant what I said. We all have our scars. We can—ah, we can only control how we—we heal from them."

That's when I am sure—in that tremble to his voice. He feels the same for me as I do for him.

My vision wavers; my head spins. I've never—I've only imagined, in words, in images, how it might feel to be this close to a boy. No, to a man. In many ways, this feels the same as being with Chloe—the crackle of charged air between us, the impossible weight that propels me toward him. But this is different, too. He is crisp lines where Chloe was gentle curves. He is structured and disciplined where Chloe was free-form frenetic energy.

I want to know both. I want to heal from the scars Chloe left on my thighs and on my heart. I want Jiro to heal them.

My breath falters; I take a step back. God. Get it together, Reiko. You are not this girl. You are not a part of this world. You have no right to interfere, to lay any sort of claim to what's happening here.

Jiro, too, exhales, but it doesn't carry the lightness of release.

"I'll be, uh . . . I'll be in my room if you need anything," I tell him. I barely hear myself say it. Embarrassment is humming along my face, heat crowding out all sense. I turn toward the door and rest my hand on the panel.

"Oh," Jiro said. "All right." His voice is tiny behind me. Then, more clearly: "But you can stay, if you like."

I slide the panel closed completely and turn back to him.

In two steps I'm standing in front of him, my lips pressed against his, so velvety and sweet. I sink to my knees as my hands cup his face; his arms wrap around my waist. He tastes like smoke and honey, rich and dark and sweet all at once; his lips feel soft as petals encompassing my own. "Miyu," he murmurs, then pulls me in for another kiss, lips parting, our mouths reaching hungrily for each other. "Miyu." When he gasps it, it sounds like a prayer or chant.

I lean against him as we kiss. He topples backward onto his pallet, still gripping me; my knees slide to either side of his waist as I pin him in place. I let my fingers trail down, against the V of his chest exposed by his robe, along the ridged, scarred flesh they find there. I kiss along his cheek and nuzzle my nose against his ear, listening to his soft gasp for breath.

His hands hook around the *obi* of my *yukata* and he glances up at me, questioning. I nod once. Yes. He tugs the sash free and slides his hands against my skin, still flush and warm from the bath. I peel his kimono open as well, sliding the thick padded shoulders off his muscled ones, and trace the old scars along his stomach. They are erratic, not orderly like my scars (*like Reiko's scars*, I think), most likely from sparring practice. But I love them. I kiss each one in turn.

Once he's undressed me fully, he kisses my stomach and runs his hand along my bare leg. His fingers pause, hesitant, at the sash wrapped around my ankle. "No," I say. Harsher than I mean. "Leave it be."

He nods. "Whatever you wish."

And so it is. He gives me all the power. I don't know what I'm doing, but I figure it out as we go, moving fluidly with him, feeling his breath and his wants and his needs and denying or allowing them as I choose. I am in control. I am the goddess I'd imagined, demanding fealty, surrendering to no one even as I give myself over to this feeling. I am glorious and he is mine and together we conquer the cold, together we heal our scars.

CHAPTER THIRTEEN

ONCE JIRO FALLS ASLEEP, I LIE AWAKE, STARING AT the ceiling of his room. As much as I want to linger with him for as long as I can, I need space to think. I need a plan. If I want to help Miyu, I have to head back into my time.

I sneak back to my quarters, untie the stone from my ankle, and fall back into myself in the present. The electronic roar of a babbling brook at my right and the heat of the toilet seat beneath me fade into existence as the scent of Jiro's skin fades out. The black stone lies on the bathroom tiles before me; I want desperately to snatch it back up, but no—there will be time for that later, when I've learned what I need to know to help Miyu.

I pull my jeans back up, then, covering my hand with my

sleeve, hurriedly wedge the stone back into my camera bag. My life here is already ended, as far as I'm concerned—ended that day I walked down the school hallways surrounded by my paintings, ended that morning I walked into Hideki's bathroom and dialed 911. The rest is just housekeeping.

I creep toward the bathroom door and listen to the voices I can still hear in the entrance of the inn. Mr. Onagi's voice is gone; now I hear Akiko and Mariko, chattering among themselves. "God, where'd she go now?" Mariko asks, exasperated in a way I've never heard her be in English. She drips with filth, like something pinched between her finger and thumb.

"Who cares?" Akiko says. "If we aren't doing a photo shoot, she can stay far, far away from me."

Mariko snorts, that awful laugh she uses only when she's trying to impress Aki. "Is everything ready for her big surprise?"

The buzzing, throbbing feeling rises in my skull. Big surprise. A big surprise for me. Somehow, I don't think it's anything good.

"Not yet," Aki says. "We should go pick up the rest of the stuff for it."

No. I don't need any of Aki's surprises. I'm not a punching bag and a scapegoat—as Reiko and as Miyu. I swing the door open and charge out into the entryway, molten lava in my veins.

What "surprise" do they have planned for me? But I can't let it show that I know.

I need to worry about planning my own surprise. A final act of vengeance at the festival, something the world will see. Mom and Dad and Hideki and Chloe and everyone else. I need to be brave and fierce, like Miyu.

I need to make them burn.

And now I'm getting the seed of an idea. My final masterpiece. I just need to see the festival layout for myself.

After giving myself a few minutes to calm my breathing and wash my face, I head back out. Aki barely spares me a second glance. "Come on. We need to head back for the afternoon rehearsal."

I nod, my face a mask, and follow our group into town. "Akiko, Akiko, Akiko!" Despite the deck being heavily stacked against him, the festival's "producer" manages to outdo Tadashi in the sleaze department. He's wearing purple pleather snakeskin pants, a double-wide-lapel button-down shirt, and a soul patch that wriggles whenever he talks like it's trying to escape its spray tan encampment. As absurd as I found Suzuki's ensemble this morning, I have to admit, she found a way to unify her look into something coherent. This guy just looks like full-frontal assault and battery made manifest.

"Hello!" Akiko says, switching rapidly into her falsetto *kawaii* voice she uses whenever she's onstage, figuratively or literally. (Right now, both.) "It's so good to see you, Franco!"

Franco swoops in for a loud, smacking kiss on the cheek, though Aki visibly recoils from the attempt with a coquettish, nervous laugh. "Listen, Aki, I am such a big fan," he says to her in Japanese, bashing his palms against his chest with the word *fan*. "A *huge fan*. Of the aki * LIFE * rhythm way. A big fan!"

Akiko titters again. "Oh, thank you, Franco—"

"No, seriously. I want you to listen to me. Your episode on spreading warmth and happiness? Changed my life. First thing I did, I turned to my assistant and gave her a pay raise. Isn't that right, Yumi?"

Yumi stares blankly at us from behind her clipboard.

"Yeah, Yumi knows. And your cover of 'Weeping in the Rain!'" Franco tosses his head back and quivers. It goes on long enough that I'm slightly concerned he may be having a seizure, but then he recovers. "Oof! It gave me such chills."

Akiko pushes a perfect curl behind one ear. "Oh, thank you, Franco. That means so much coming from you."

Franco tosses his hands up and sways back and forth. He looks like the girls who always got way too into the hymns at Saint Isaac's. "Aki, life, rhythm!" Franco sings as he rocks his hips. "Aki, life—*RHYTHM*!" He punches forward.

"So, uhm . . ." Akiko takes a step back. "How do you want me to do this?"

"Right! The show." Franco claps, then spins toward poor Yumi. "Yumi, c'mere, let's block this out."

I sigh and flick my snapshot camera off. This will take some time.

Kenji laughs beside me, a quiet laugh meant for just the two of us. "I'm guessing you don't know anything about Franco."

"I feel like I know him pretty well already," I say.

Kenji grins. "He is a former mid-list *aidoru*. And a mid-list character actor . . . and a mediocre fashion designer . . . also a pretty terrible restaurateur." He ticks each of these professions off on his fingers, then wiggles his thumb. "Now he's a disaster of a special events planner and promoter, which is why he and Tadashi get along so well."

"One of those perpetual motion machines of marginal fame," I say. "Yeah, we have a few of those in the States, too." When Kenji looks confused, I explain perpetual motion machines to him in English. I have to stop myself from switching into Japanese. "I'm sure he and Akiko are going to get along just fine."

"Seriously? Look at her. Even Aki has some standards." Kenji gestures to where she's side by side with Franco, looking at the rig for a massive drum ensemble, trying to edge out of the arm he's slung around her shoulders. It's almost enough to make me feel sorry for the girl.

Almost.

I study the drum rigging, tiered behind the stage like the setup for a percussive choir. In the metal bar rafters of the stage, dozens and dozens of stage lights cram tight, like they've packed the setup for a massive opera hall onto this tiny rig. And tangled around everything are the same colored fabric banners, flapping every which way, just like they were in Miyu's version of Kuramagi.

The flapping, tangled-up, dangerously flammable colored banners.

My arms tingle like they've fallen asleep. Franco's nonstop prattling blurs into a dim, distant drone. Kenji's explaining something to me, something that actually has to do with our job here, but I don't hear it. All I can feel is the rushing heat of fire and the angry pulse of the drums. I want this. I want this so badly, and I feel no semblance of remorse.

Akiko deserves to pay—for humiliating me, for mocking me, for plotting even more humiliations yet to come. Laughter rings in my head, something that sounds like me, though I can't remember the last time I've laughed. This feeling unfurling within me, catching the wind of my hate like a sail, feels so goddamned good it's better than sex with Jiro, it's better than food, it's better than slicing open my skin and airing all my scars.

The perfect revenge, perfectly planned, perfectly formed.

Dimly, I hear the buzzing in my head once more. I imagine wasps raging inside my stomach. I imagine roaches crawling along my skin. I imagine the blood and entrails dripping down the side of my face, and I wear them like a medal.

I'll bring the lights down on Aki. So easy to make it look like an accident, like I was just setting things up for a photo shoot. But it'll go horribly awry. Set fire to the stage. Chaos.

Blood. Screaming. Her dream chance turned to a nightmare. How I can't wait.

The drums echo in my brain as the plan forms, as I chart everything I'll need to do to set it up. It won't take much. So easy. So easy.

The revenge we're owed.

The thought comes to me all at once, but it feels so right. I deserve this.

"Reiko?"

Kenji's saying my name. Maybe has been for some time. I turn toward Kenji, irritation itchy as wool against my flesh. "What?"

He shrinks back. "I, uh, just—you had this—sorry. You had this look on your face, and I wanted to make sure you felt—"

"Felt what?" I snarl.

"Reiko!" Aki shouts at me from the stage. "Are you even paying attention?"

I level my gaze right at Aki and Franco. Franco's smile is gone; even his soul patch is still. "Don't you worry, Aki," I shout back at her. "It's going to be a perfect show."

CHAPTER FOURTEEN

HAS VENGEANCE ALWAYS BEEN IN MY BLOOD? I'M
starting to think so.

I study the festival stage and the metal scaffolding that
supports the lights. They're older lights, like the kind in Saint
Isaac's auditorium, not the sleek modern ones we had at the
summer arts camp. Every year the fire marshall fined our
school when he did his inspection before the spring musical.
I never paid it much mind back then; my job was as the official photographer, posting shots from dress rehearsal to the
school's Facebook page.

But now his words come back to me. *Aging filaments. Easy
to catch fire,* he'd say, shaking his head. *You drop one of these*

on the stage, it's not just the weight that'll hurt you. It's far too easy for it to catch and spread.

I snap a few photographs of the winches that hold it in place. Old metal, oxidized and soft. The stage managers have plenty of timed catch-release devices set aside in a box; Aki's even going to use a few to drop banners and confetti during her big finale.

"Are you okay?" Kenji asks, breaking me from my reverie.

I blink a few times and realize I was smiling.

Vengeance. My blood. My birthright. Just like Hideki and me. He inflicted a thousand tiny torments on me over the years, but I'll get mine in the end.

"I feel amazing," I say.

◈

By the time Aki's rehearsal is finished, my plan is set. I head back to the *ryokan* to gather the final pieces I need while the others head to dinner or to the *onsen* to relax in the hot springs. I assemble everything I'll need for tomorrow. I have a plan. I will make sure everyone knows my name.

But there is another kind of determination thrumming through me, and I'm not ready to settle in for the night. I shed my clothes and dress for the hot springs. Something in me wants to feel the burn and sting of the water; something in me is pushing me on.

I am surrounded by the buzzing. It carries me forward, like a tidal wave. Urges me onto the streets, onto the path to the *onsen*s.

The sun is spilling across the edge of the western mountains like a runny yolk, all oranges and yellows that I'd love to capture in my DSLR camera, but I'm on a mission this evening. My feet carry me as if on their own volition. The wooden sandals feel like second nature now, the slow shuffle and scrape; the white and blue *yukata* feels like a second skin. I've never felt so alive—not in any recent memory, that's for sure. Invigorated.

I can't stop to question it or the moment will be gone. I'm slipping away, watching my body surge forth. Letting this rotten core within me take control. And it feels so good. It feels like what I've been reaching for all along.

I unlatch the gate and slip into the outer garden of the private *onsen* Mr. Onagi owns. Clack, clack my way into the wooden bathhouse. A sign warns me the *onsen* is already occupied, but I pay it no mind. I'm an electric arc of energy that can't be stopped. Shed my outer robe and shoes. Rinse myself off in the shower stand in the bathhouse corner. Then slide open the doorway and step out into the inner courtyard, where the sunken hot spring sits, offering a beautiful view of the valley beyond under the final throes of the sunset.

Where Kenji sits, naked, inside the spring.

"Oh—oh." He scrambles backward, water flying, and curls up at the far end of the stone basin. "Hi, um, Reiko. What are you, um, doing—doing here?"

He tries to keep his gaze down, but I can feel it—I feel it feathering along the bony ridges of my ribs, my shrunken breasts, the stretch marks around my stomach. It trips up on the rows and rows of scars, those dark gray furrows against the lighter skin of my thighs. I step toward the edge of the pool, letting the steam snake up around me and greet me like an old lover. It smells faintly of sulfur, just enough to wake me up.

I am alive. I am so alive. No one can stop me.

I sink one foot into the basin, then the next. The scalding water is as hot as a slap against bare skin. I feel like I'm being roasted alive. It's wonderful. It feels so angry, so vicious, like the water's defending itself against intruders. But I am winning.

I always win.

I don't know where the thought comes from, but I am so certain of it that it must be true. I always win in the end. I always have my revenge. And I'm going to have it again.

"Don't you ever wonder," I ask Kenji, who's still curled up at the far end of the pool, "what happens to our pain when we die?" I'm not quite sure where the question comes from— but I like the molten way it tastes in my mouth. "Maybe it lasts and lasts. It powers the earth and heats these springs." I tilt my head. "Wouldn't that be nice?"

"I, uh, I'm not sure what you're talking ab—wait." Kenji squints at me; for a moment, his arms unfold from his legs, and I can glimpse the murky expanse of his chest and stomach beneath the rocking, fracturing surface of the water. "You're—you're speaking Japanese."

"Am I?" I ask. Then I'm laughing—I recognize the laugh like something I heard in a movie once, something that feels familiar and yet foreign. "I guess there's a lot you don't know about me."

Yes. Yes, this is me. The water is burning away everything I used to be—weak, ugly, cowardly, hated. What remains is only what truly matters. My power. My hate.

"Rei?" It's Kenji. Looking at me with eyes rounded in fear. He should be afraid. Everyone should. "What's going on with you, Rei?"

I shove off the bottom of the pool and lurch toward him. "Isn't this what you wanted, Kenji?" My voice flows from me like honey. I remember Jiro's face as he caressed my skin. I can make Kenji do that, too. I have that power. "It's why you asked me, right? Earlier today."

Kenji's face darkens, and he lowers his hands to try to conceal himself. As if I give a shit about modesty.

"No need to hide. I know it. You want me like this." I try

to crouch in front of him, but my toes slip on the stone floor of the basin. I stretch one hand toward him, run my fingers along his cheeks. "You want me like I want you."

"I—uhh, umm—" He shrinks back from my touch, head pressing against the stone ledge of the pool. "I really like you, Rei, but I don't think either of us—I mean, I don't think this is—"

Anger flares through me. I imagine the water boiling around me. Boiling us alive. "You don't think *what?*" I snarl.

"You're not acting like yourself." Kenji gulps, loud.

I seize his knee in one hand and shove it out of my way. Swim over him, my face looming before his. Yes, he wants me. "Don't be stupid." And I want to devour him whole. "I've never been so . . . me."

He slides one hand between us. "Seriously. I'm in no rush—this isn't the way I want—"

I grip him by his shoulders. Why is he being so stupid? Why fight? I am power, I am divine. How dare he reject me?

Kenji shoves me—hard, hands right in the center of my chest, pushing against my solar plexus. The wind rushes out of me as I go drifting to the other side of the pool. It *hurts.* "Who are you?" he cries. "Who are you, seriously? Because this isn't the girl I've been getting to know." Stars swim before my eyes as I try to right myself. Kenji stands up, water sliding off him; he's shaking. "The Reiko I know would actually *listen* to me."

"What the hell are you talking about?" He doesn't understand. I've never been so *alive*. Of course he doesn't know how that feels. I'm so hungry for life, for making use of this gift, this incredible power I feel coursing through me, to command everyone, to avenge everything.

Kenji is nothing. I need more. I need better. I need . . .

Suddenly all the fight drains out of me. The confidence is gone. I look at Kenji, and I see fear in his eyes. He's looking at me the way Chloe did. After I'd already done what couldn't be undone.

Oh, God. Oh, God. What have I become?

Steam rises from my body, swirling around me like a fog. I need to get back to Miyu.

"Rei?" Kenji calls to me, as I head back into the bathhouse. "Rei? Talk to me. Are you—are you sure you're okay?"

I wrap my *yukata* around me—left over right, the *correct* way that I learned from being Miyu, despite what Aki told me in the past—and stomp away from him while he's still scrambling to get dressed.

No. I'm not okay. I weave back through the streets of Kuramagi with fire in my veins. Night's dropped swiftly across the village, dampening everything into blackness punctuated only by the golden pockets of the paper lanterns every twenty feet or so. My sandals scrape scrape along, ringing through the night. Two older tourists stumble from an *izakaya*, laughing, but the laughter fades as they catch sight of me, and they hurry down the other way.

Is that my heartbeat throbbing in my head? Buzzing around me? No—no, I hear it now. The drums. Practicing for tomorrow's festival. But they feel like a warning. I have to get away from those drums. I plunge into the swirl of shadows around the staircase that takes me back up to the *ryokan*.

The shadows are thick, congealing like a stew around me. For a moment, I can't see anything but blackness. Can't hear anything but those drums. The only thing I feel is the sizzle under my skin, the yearning to break free.

The yearning for revenge. On Kenji and Akiko and Miyu's tormentors, all tangled into one.

I will have it. I'll have my revenge.

Tomorrow is the festival, Aki's big day. But it will be mine. And then I can go back to where I belong.

CHAPTER FIFTEEN

MOST OF THE LIGHTS ARE OUT IN THE PUBLIC SPACES of the *ryokan*; Sierra hunches over a logbook, illuminated by a single desk lamp. "Oh, hey, Reiko," she says, starting to look up as I kick the wooden sandals into a far cubby. "—Oh. Hey. Are you, um . . . Is everything okay?"

I stare at her for a few seconds, trying to parse out her words from the buzzing in my head. I blink. "I'm fine." Why does everyone keep asking me that? What's so fundamentally wrong with the way I look, the way I am, that I have to constantly be checked on? Don't treat me like I'm back in the goddamned psych ward. Don't send your little orderlies around to check on me. Don't send Kenji to spy on me, to keep me from hurting myself or others.

I don't even feel the urge to hurt myself anymore. I deserve better.

It's everyone else who needs to feel pain.

"Well, where are the rest of your friends?" Sierra asks. "It's only an hour until curfew. Mr. Onagi knows they've been sneaking out."

I tilt my head, transfixed by her lips, so lush and velvety as she talks. I imagine how they might feel searing a path down my neck, the way Chloe's once did. Only a day off the meds, and I've finally thawed out the ice that had sealed my libido away. I take a step toward the desk. I could seize her chin in one hand, guide her face toward mine. Just because Kenji's a coward doesn't mean Sierra will be, too.

"*Reiko.*" She says it urgently, but not with the passion I'd hoped for. "Listen. You *need* to get your friends back here."

I feel my lips smiling, crackling with ice. "They deserve to suffer."

The smooth line of her throat ripples as she swallows hard. All of her muscles have turned stiff; she's gripping something in one hand. "This isn't a joke. This village, it—" Her grip slackens by a fraction, and I can see what she's holding now. A letter opener. "It does things. It's not a good place. The festival, they hold it every year for the priests to purify the town, but we all have to do our part."

A frown creases my face. She's holding the letter opener

like she thinks she needs to protect herself. From what? From *me*? "What do you mean, it does things?"

"Something terrible happened. A long time ago." She presses the letter opener back onto the desk, but her fingertips keep moving along it, like it's an agitated animal she's trying to calm. "I don't know what, no one will say. I just know how it feels when you walk the village streets at night."

The drums. The whispers. The shadows that swirl and shift like fog. And the earthquake, unleashing its primal howl. "You don't strike me as the superstitious sort," I say.

Sierra smiles. She's looking more like herself again; something's put her at ease. Maybe she wasn't afraid of me. I no longer feel the same buzzing in my head, but I can feel it coiled up, waiting for me back in its nest. I smile back at her, suddenly feeling a little silly for how I've been acting.

Relax, Reiko. It's just been a strange day. But I barely remember it. All I recall is Jiro's bare skin warm against mine—

"I'm not, not really. But living here—it's hard not to, you know? There's a bad energy lurking around Kuramagi." Sierra's hand finally leaves the letter opener, and she scratches the back of her head. "But hey, the festival helps, and it's almost time for it, right? Get everything all purified once more."

Purify. The word sends a thrill down my spine. Yes. I want to be purified. I want to cleanse these streets. The humming starts up again.

Sierra's saying something. I stare at her teeth, like maybe the words will be scrawled across them in some language I can understand. But they're all just words, dumb words, English or Japanese, I don't even care. All I hear are drums. Maybe she's asking me something. Maybe there's something I need to do for her. Sierra. A pretty name. I do like her, or I did; but that's unimportant now. I don't need her or Kenji or anyone else.

Miyu has the answers.

Miyu is my future. My purification.

Sierra shouts after me as I turn and head for the stairs.

❖

As soon as I step back into Miyu, I can tell something's changed. My stomach twists as I try to adjust, but there are lights, there are voices, there are too many people crammed around me, pointing and talking with strange muffled tones—

I've come into Miyu mid-conversation with no clues about what's going on. I blink, trying to see past the harsh syrupy light that hardens and casts everyone around me in amber. I recognize Miyu's father at one end of the low table where we all huddle around, but I don't know any of the other faces. They wear drab farmer's clothes or the garb of clerks—maybe they are the *daimyo*'s attendants.

Then I glance overhead at the peaked roof so low above us. Ahh. We are in the secret room.

Father and his co-conspirators.

"—and if the soldiers are watching this side alley, like Miyu claims . . ." Father gestures to the rough sketch spread on the table before us. Slowly, the hatch marks and symbols on it begin to make sense. It's a model of the village square, and the streets immediately surrounding it.

"How can we trust her word?" The man to my father's right asks—a rounded, lopsided man, with one eye that rolls like a fish. "She's never kept it before."

I itch to feel a blade's hilt in my palm. I itch to see the rivulets of red.

"Even a cowardly dog has its uses," Father says, words falling like a gavel. "And my daughter will have hers."

I don't feel half as grateful to him as I suspect I am supposed to.

When the man says nothing else, my father continues. "—So our best place to position is here, along the secondary path. They will be coming along the guarded one, but we'll have the advantage of height. We can inflict great damage before we are spotted."

"No. It's not enough." It's Yodo speaking—the only other woman around the table. "Great damage is not all we are aiming for. We'll have to draw the soldiers away, when it is too late for them to communicate orders to hold off."

The man to Yodo's left, wispy and gray-haired, nods. "We need a distraction."

My muscles tense as I study the map. They are planning something for the festival—that much is obvious. But what? It almost looks like they are trying to seal off the square. But they are also talking about bringing something into the square. What are they after?

"Perhaps," the round man says, "this is the perfect occasion for our cowardly dog."

All eyes turn toward me.

"Miyu." There is no warmth in my father's tone as he speaks; if anything, he stinks of desperation. "We need you to make this happen."

"No. Absolutely not." The round man bashes his fist against the table. "She was born with failure wrapped around her throat. She killed your wife on her way out of the womb and she's been a harbinger of failure, an ill omen, ever since."

So that explains some of my father's hatred for me, then. I shrink back, my anger momentarily quelled. But it comes roaring back almost immediately. How dare they blame me for my mother's death? As if it is some sort of choice I made— something I had control over! I clench one hand into a fist and drive my knuckles against my thigh. I hate them. I hate all of them. They deserve to pay.

"I know what she has done." My father's gaze never leaves my face; it is steady as a surgeon's knife, peeling back all the layers of my skin. For a moment it almost feels as if he can see past Miyu entirely, to me, Reiko, underneath. "And so does everyone else in this village. That's why she's the perfect distraction."

The perfect distraction. Oh, but I am so much more than a momentary diversion. I can do so much worse.

"Fine. But if we get disemboweled because your idiot girl couldn't do anything right—" the round man starts.

But Father raises his hand. "Miyu will play her part. She knows better than to fail me again." He stares right through me. "You will cause a scene in the square on my signal. Understood?"

I nod, sharp. "As my father commands, so shall I obey."

I make my way down toward my room, one of the first to trickle out of the hidden chamber—we spread out our departures, so as not to rouse the samurai from their sleep. Not that we need to be concerned—the snores coming from their room are powerful enough to rattle the wooden panels in their tracks. Goemon's doing, I have no doubt. I round the corner into my room—and nearly scream as I run right into Jiro.

He throws his arms around me. "Shh, shh, it's only me. I'm sorry." He helps me into my room and slides the panel closed behind him. "I didn't mean to startle you. I only . . . I wanted to see your face."

Yes. This is the response I deserve—someone eager to see

me, hungry for whatever I give them. Not like Kenji. Not like Sierra, who has no need to be afraid. More proof that this is the world I belong in. I cradle my fingertips along Jiro's jawline and pull him in for a kiss, desperate and starving.

He sinks down beside me on my pallet, and we kiss each other as if we've been away for years, not hours. How quickly I've come to feel for him—for this whole strange world—in a way that I can never seem to muster for my own life. I no longer care how Miyu feels about me taking over her body, her life. I've earned this. I deserve to have a life that is actually worth living.

I tug at the V of Jiro's collar and nibble at his collarbone. He stifles a laugh. "No. No, Miyu. Wait. There's—there's something I want to speak to you about."

I pause. Words like that usually send a shock of ice through my veins. But he is still smiling, still holding me close to him. "You have my attention," I tell him. "As always."

He smiles and brushes a stray wisp of hair back from my face. "I'm thinking of leaving the shogun's service. Forsaking my income, my standing in the samurai. Washing my hands of the whole *bakufu* government."

I tighten my grip on the hem of his robe. Abandon the shogunate and the way of the blade. Is he really willing to do that? But then I recall what he said about the samurai's path being meaningless these days. Either they are clerks, like he and Goemon, sent on endless pointless errands, or they are frightful bullies, like the *shinsengumi* who roam the country-side sowing terror and compliance. Jiro deserves better than either of those paths.

"Is that . . . is it really safe for you to do so?" I ask. "You'd become *ronin*—masterless. Doesn't it betray your code?"

"I'd rather have no master than serve one I don't believe in. But it does present some . . . challenges." His jaw sets in a hard line. "There are still some details I must figure out. But yes, I think it can be done. Maybe. I don't know." He winces, and curls forward, nose pressing against my throat as he plants a fresh kiss there. "All I know is, I can't keep on this current path. It isn't the life I want. And I think . . . I think this isn't the life that you want, either."

It is all I can do not to laugh at that. If he only knew how badly I want Miyu's life instead of my own. But he has a point—Miyu, and me as Miyu, deserve better than to be her father's and her village's whipping post. Whatever she has done, it's not worth their hate. It is time for her to become something more.

"You're better than this tiny place. Its simple grudges and narrow-minded ways." Jiro kisses me again, and then sucks at my exposed flesh, sending a hot flare of desire straight through me. I curve toward him with an unbidden moan. He kisses back up to my jawline, then pulls back to stare me right in the eye. "What if we could escape?"

I pause. "Together, you mean."

Jiro nods, squeezing me closer. He smells so comforting—of pine and plums, of a hearth in wintertime. "Yes. Together."

I tightened my embrace. He is a man of keen edges but a soft heart. A blade when he has to be, but otherwise, a safe haven. This is so different from losing myself in Chloe. This isn't expecting someone else to save me. This is someone opening the door for me, showing me the path to my own salvation.

All he did is give me the opportunity. It is for me to take.

But I hesitate. My situation here is precarious. If I ever lost the rock . . .

Yet if I can find a way to make this more permanent, to somehow isolate myself back in my world so I can be free to live Miyu's life for the rest of my days . . . There had to be a way. I have to think of something.

"I understand. It's a big decision. You don't have to decide right now." Jiro kisses me again, and slides one hand to cup the back of my thigh. "But don't think too long. I'm afraid I have to leave soon. I'd just . . ." His sigh aches right through me, stoking the fire in my gut. "I'd rather not go without you."

"I'll let you know as soon as I can," I tell him honestly. And then I surrender to his touch once more, our muffled sighs concealing the faintest shuffle of bare feet as Father's conspirators trickle out into the night.

❖

For the first time in forever, I wonder how I might make a collage again. How would I frame Kenji? He'd have to be hunched over his sketchpad, with a cascade of color and life roiling out of the pad like a rogue wave. Blues and golds and purples spilling over the canvas, dwarfing his black-and-white shape. I'd put him off center, to show him escaping the rigid school system and the even more rigid animation studios and art collectives he wants nothing to do with.

Sierra's canvas, too, would glow from within. Her mint-green nails would jump off the canvas, and I'd pepper the blank space with gold leaf. Weave in photographs from all over the world to match her wanderlust. A hand reaching out, warm, just waiting to be grasped.

The village of Kuramagi, though, would be a closed-off image. Locked up gates, buried power lines, lists of rules that cannot be bent. The image grows and grows in my mind, like poisoned water seeping into the ground from a dark well. A dark shadow locked away here, and every attempt to contain it makes it thicker, heavier, collapsing in on itself.

❖

Afterward, I return to my time, and stare into the darkness of our room back at the *ryokan*, fingertips resting just beyond the stone. The room is silent, but I'm gasping for breath; all the thoughts in my head are crowding around, pulling tight like a noose around me. I need to make a plan. Something permanent. *Do it. You can run. You can leave your life behind. Surrender this life. Live a long and full life as Miyu instead; abandon your broken body and broken world for good . . .*

I just need a plan. I need guarantees. So far, it doesn't seem like any time passes at all in my world when I'm inhabiting Miyu's, but what if that's not true over a longer period of time? Say, years? What if someone takes the stone out of my grip?

And say I did live out Miyu's life—say she lived to eighty, to ninety. A long and fulfilling life. When it comes to its end, will I wake up right here in Kuramagi, still eighteen years old, still waiting to get dragged along to Akiko's performance at the cultural festival? No. I can't face that. I came here barely wanting to live one life—I definitely don't want to live two.

I hear voices outside, in the garden below. I can't make out what they are saying but I know I hear my name. It snares me like a fishing hook, and I am unable to resist. I slide out of bed, slowly, quietly, and creep toward the window without ever rising up high enough to show my face.

"—telling you, there's something wrong with her. Really, really wrong." Kenji's voice, shaky and uncertain. He's trying to keep it down as he speaks in Japanese.

"Of course there is. She's *Reiko*," Akiko's voice replies. "You should see her giant bag of pills. The ridiculous 'instruction manual' her parents sent us when she came over. Runs on her father's side of the family, I guess—she didn't get it from ours. Her brother tried to kill himself, you know. And they say she threatened her classmates."

"Yes—yes, I know about her brother, her hospital stay. I know she's been—struggling for a while. But this is something different." Kenji's trying so hard to speak quietly. Idiot. "She came to me in the *onsen*, and there was something about the way she was moving, the way she talked—it's like she wasn't herself at all—"

"Wait, did she try to seduce you?" Akiko's laugh punctures the still night. "That's hilarious! Tell me more!"

What the hell is Kenji talking about? I never—
Wait.

I remember now. I remember the steam whispering against my bare skin and Kenji pushing me away. God, it feels like a lifetime ago, like a grainy camera phone video I watched of someone else's life.

What was I thinking, trying to seduce Kenji? Sure, I felt something for him before, the faintest of flutter that could penetrate my medicated haze, but I never really wanted Kenji. I just want Jiro. I just want . . .

The buzzing in my head turns ravenous, angry. Still, Kenji was a fool to deny me. Can't he see me, the power I have? My vengeance won't spare him, I decide, as red wreathes my vision once more. The fire in me grows and grows.

"This isn't funny, Aki." Kenji's adamant now, speaking

louder despite himself. "There's something wrong here—really wrong. The look she had in her eyes . . ." His voice drops once more, quavering. "I'm scared of what she might do."

Oh, poor, foolish Kenji. He's right to be scared. They all are. But they have no idea why—not yet.

Soon enough, though, I'll make them all see. The buzzing inside of me answers like a happy sigh. Everything is coming together.

Footsteps on the stairs jar me back to myself. Someone's coming up to the room. I scramble back into bed and squeeze my eyes shut just as the panel slides open and the sound of two slippers getting kicked aside rings out. Someone huffs into the room. "Rei? You here?" Mariko asks, in English. "Are you awake?"

I don't answer. I have nothing to say to her. No use for her at all.

Mariko sighs and pads over to the mini fridge. I tense. I'm practically vibrating with anticipation—yes. Eat your stupid *onigiri*. Darkness swirls on the backs of my eyelids, the humming swells, I feel like an insect about to split open, all my innards spilling over—

Then Aki enters the room. "Ugh. You're eating again?"

Mariko hesitates. "Well, you said we can't go to the club tonight . . . I thought it would be okay . . ."

"Quit whining. You saw what a creep Franco is. He's just

going to harass me all night if we go. Besides, I need my beauty rest."

"Tomorrow's going to be awesome," Mariko says, in her fakest, cheeriest tone.

Aki leans over near me and starts digging through her suitcase in search of her pajamas. I shut my eyes again.

Then I hear it. The crinkle, crinkle of the wrapper as Mariko tears open the seaweed sheath and then wraps it around the triangle of rice. My skin is on fire. Yes. Yes.

Crunch.

The sound of Mariko's chewing fills the tiny, silent room.

I feel like I've just run a marathon—exhausted and pumped and flush with achievement. But I also want more. This is just the first, tantalizing hit of my revenge. There's so much more to come. Tomorrow will be perfection. Everything is falling into place.

Then I can see about taking Miyu's place permanently.

CHAPTER SIXTEEN

I DREAM OF A SHARP BLADE POKING INTO MY BACK. A threat lingering over me like a shadow. But I am anger and crisp edges, I am lashing out, I am a rabid animal who's been backed into a corner too many times. No one can stop me now. I will tear them all apart in their fall.

I wake up gasping for breath. I'm certain I'm drowning—that someone's holding me down. I swear I can feel water burning in my lungs as I try to suck down air. But it's just our room. There's no one around.

Akiko and Mariko are already gone. Their pallets look slept in, and the aroma of perfume and deodorant hangs in the air. Hopefully they're at breakfast, then, or have set off for the festival without me. I have lots to do to prepare for the festival, but first, I need to get back to Miyu. Tell Jiro I've made my decision to run away with him.

The stone is still wedged down underneath my sheets. With a sigh of relief, I wrap my fingers around it and sink into its heat.

❖

I am standing at the front windows of the *honjin*, a cleaning rag in my hand—I must have stumbled upon Miyu in the midst of her daily wipe-down of the walls. Colored paper streamers adorn the shops across the street, and the people flowing from the shrine nearby wear their finest robes— luxurious silk with brilliant pops of turquoise, pink, and navy for the women and blues and grays for the men. Behind me, I heard Goemon's barking tone pontificating about something or another; I don't bother to strain to hear the words. Probably something about the festival.

I recall Father's command—my duty is to cause a distraction during the festivities. I shrugged it off before as Miyu's job, and not mine. But now this is my price of admission for entering Miyu's world. If I'm to take her place, then I must do so fully, and that means keeping her promises.

Hooves thunder on the cobblestones; the crowd parts and cheers as a procession of horses plow down the street. Some part of me recognizes the crest fluttering on the banners: the *daimyo*'s house.

Our feudal lord has returned from Kyoto to take part in the festival.

My chest feels tighter and tighter as I wipe down the wood; I am trying to maneuver all the puzzle pieces into place. Father is loyal to the *daimyo*, who is loyal to the emperor. Miyu understands that much. But I also know what the historian at the *honjin* said—that those who backed the emperor over the shogunate did so at great risk. Goemon and Jiro serve the shogunate, so Father is at odds with them, and we are keeping Father's plans to attack someone from them.

But who does Father mean to attack? What's happening at the festival?

Jiro cares nothing for these stupid politics—it's why he wants to flee. I'm not going to trust him with Father's plans—I recognize my own ignorance enough not to do that—but surely he won't stop them. Like me, he's been an impartial participant. The role I play is strictly for Miyu's benefit, which is soon to be mine.

The processional halts, and two men climb from the litters—one my father's age, another a few years older than me, clutching his belly as they strut bow-legged up the *honjin*'s path. The younger one's upper lip curls back in disgust as he studies the *honjin*'s exterior, and he turns to the older man: "How long must we stay here again?"

"Not long at all." The older man grins. "Soon we'll be riding triumphantly back to Kyoto."

Father and Yodo rush out of the kitchen to greet the *daimyo*; I start a new row of polishing, but Father hisses at me and beckons me to his side. "Miyu!" Father cries. I rush toward him, and we all line up and kneel in a row as the *daimyo* struts inside, apprising us. With a nod, he bids us to rise.

"You recall the *daimyo*, the most esteemed and wise Lord Yoshida-dono," Father says. His anxious face and glowering eyes urge me to drop into another kneel, so I do. "And his second eldest son. Tsurube-sama."

Tsurube. At the name, a wave of cold creeps over Miyu's body. From what little I've heard while occupying Miyu, I have a pretty good idea who Tsurube is meant to be.

My betrothed.

Tsurube—the pot-bellied man, his eyes like hateful little beads, looks me over with a gaze like a rake. "Huh. From the stories of her infamy, I was expecting more." He chuckles to himself, then turns to his father, Lord Yoshida. "You said I needn't give up my girls back in Kyoto, right?"

Father clears his throat as my mouth flaps open. Hatred boiled up inside me—I lust to see his hideous face bashed in—but Father speaks before I can. "It is my daughter's deepest honor to bear you your heirs, Lord Tsurube-san," Father says. "As it is your prerogative as lord to remain virile and strong however you choose."

Translation: husbands can screw around with whomever they want, while wives are honor-bound to be faithful. Yeah, I am getting the hang of old Japanese real quick.

Tsurube nods with another phlegmy laugh. "Then yes, I think she will do."

Both Father and Yoshida are nearly limp with relief. "Wonderful," Yoshida says. "Come, then. Let us discuss the specifics of the . . . festival."

The look that passes between them leaves no doubt in my mind which specifics they mean.

As soon as their backs are turned, I storm for my room. No. No. I can't marry that slug. As soon as my promise to Father is completed, I can run away with Jiro.

"Hey. Hey, are you all right?" Jiro catches me by the shoulders as I turn toward my room. "Miyu." His voice drops. "What's the matter?"

I clench my teeth. "Nothing. It won't matter any longer."

His eyes search mine; his face is tense, stony, nothing like the soft lips I'd lost myself in the night before. "Miyu . . . who was that arrogant monster?" he asks.

I have to look away. "My husband to be."

Jiro flinches; his whole body clenches up. "And you're going to—"

"No. Absolutely not." I take a deep breath. "I've made up my mind. I'm coming with you."

Jiro grips my face and kisses me. I could melt into that kiss forever and stay lost in it. He must feel the same way; his lips linger, and he slowly pries himself back. "All right. I think I have a plan."

❖

"Reiko! Reiko, wake up! Come on, you're going to miss it!"

I blink against the harsh overhead lights, the glaring sun. Where's the stone? All these faces are crowded around me, blurring together; a forest of legs surrounds me. I shove blindly at them. Shit. I'm not ready—I need to go back to Jiro. We have to finish making our plans. I toss back the duvet coverlet, but I can't find the stone in the bedding.

Oh, God. Panic pins me in place. I have to get back to Miyu. I have to fulfill her promise to her father and then run away with Jiro—

I didn't get to hear Jiro's plan—

Aki's voice stabs through my frantic thoughts. "Welcome, everyone, to aki * LIFE * rhythm! Today's the big day—the cultural festival in the village of Kuramagi. And to show you how easy it is to integrate the aki * LIFE * rhythm system into your own style, I'm going to be giving a surprise makeover to the Team Aki photographer, Reiko Azumi!"

I can't move. Slowly, horribly, the glare of lights in my face recede enough for the scene before me to come into focus:

Kazuo and Tadashi hunch over my pallet, each with camcorders in their hands. And Akiko crouches beside me, fully made up, perfectly dressed, wearing her camera-ready smile.

Akiko's surprise for me. Her horrible, awful surprise.

"Reiko's style is sad. Frumpy. Lonely!" As Aki talks, I can already hear the blipping sound effects Kazuo's going to add to the footage in post-production. "She's lost her love for life. She's lost her rhythm. But no matter!" Aki bounces onto her feet. "Team Aki is here to help!"

"No. No, no, no. Please leave me alone—" But my tongue rolls useless in my mouth. My arms and legs are numb; my head is fuzzy, so fuzzy, I can hardly think. This is worse than my deepest benzo-induced haze. Like I'm having an out-of-body experience—like I'm already watching this whole horrible tableau play out on YouTube, unable to intervene.

I can't think; I can't move. Too many thoughts are cramming into my head. I can't get them out of me, can't escape their constant buzz. They build and build and build, solidifying, until finally they are a single message:

We will have our revenge together. We are one.

One. Relief washes over me, cooling down my anger. Yes. Miyu has been with me all along. She knows my pain and I know hers. Together, we can end it.

I can endure this. Our revenge is coming soon. I can face one last humiliation.

Then Akiko is through.

They scrub my skin with exfoliants. Rip the blackheads from my pores. Slather some sort of Korean slug oil all over my face. Pluck and wax and tone. Mariko first straightens my hair, then curls it, then piles it atop my head while Akiko demonstrates proper eyeliner technique, and she explains, "For all those poor souls like Reiko who weren't born with the double eyelid fold." *Yeah, right*, I think. Like a surgeon didn't create Aki's.

"And if you have a sickly body type, like Reiko, remember—softer definition is your friend! We want you to look huggable, not prickly. Soft without looking overweight."

They swaddle me up in historically inaccurate underclothes for a kimono—Miyu would be mortified—and stick the accoutrements in my hair. Blood red stain across my lips. Finally, the silk kimono, feeling cheap and flimsy compared to what Miyu usually wears. "And there you have it—the Aki LIFE style! Traditional and modern—perfect for YOUR life and YOUR rhythm."

My life. My rhythm. The drumbeats goad me on, darker and darker, and my smile spreads.

Akiko leads us from the *ryokan* toward the trail we took on our first day here, the one that leads to the lovers' shrine. Time for a photo shoot, now that we're all made up and wearing traditional gear. "Today is a celebration of tradition, but also with a dash of modernity. With aki * LIFE * rhythm, we embrace our past while dancing forward into a beautiful future. And I'm going to show you how!"

The mythical shrine at last—looks like they sent Kenji ahead to find the right path for us this time. Two battered fingers of greenish stone stand side by side, nearly six feet tall, yoked together by an ancient, fraying rope. Paper cranes clutter the base of the monoliths. Apparently it's not a formal Shinto shrine, but something more organic, taking on a life of its own. The cranes, scrawled with prayers and wishes, tell a tale of desperation, of hundreds and hundreds of pilgrims casting their lot with whomever the two stupid lovers were who felt like some ugly rocks in the ground were the best way to commemorate their love.

"And now, my dear aki * LIFE * rhythm fans, it's time to hear the sad tale of the lovers. One to rival dear Ohatsu and Tokubei in the *Love Suicides at Sonezaki*. Once upon a time, during the shogun's rule, this shrine was built in memory of two lovers in the village." Aki strikes a *kawaii* pose in front of the stone. Snap, snap goes Kenji's camera flash. "They were so very much in love, but sadly, they could not be together in this world! Their social standing would not allow it. C'mon, Reiko, pose," she adds, hissing the last under her breath. "So they made a lovers' suicide pact—a *shinju*. Their deaths in this world would reunite them in the world beyond and free them from the order that kept them apart. Now, I don't know if that's true or not, but it has certainly immortalized their love here, for us in this life! So romantic, right?"

Snap, snap.

Two lovers who couldn't be together in this life.

Flashes blotting out my sight.

They were so very much in love.

I am like a cockroach, splitting open, my guts pouring out. I am a sliced-open stomach, dangling with entrails. Once upon a time, during the shogun's rule. The memories overwhelm me, vivid and hot as blood. Are they Miyu's memories? I don't remember falling, but I remember how it feels—it feels like someone stoking the fading embers of my heart.

I know. I don't know how, but I know. It has to be.

The lovers who failed in their quest to escape the status quo must be Miyu and Jiro.

CHAPTER SEVENTEEN

I CATCH MYSELF ON THE MOSSY GREEN ALTAR STONES. Their cold seeps like acid against my skin. I push away from them, and shove through the wall of Tadashi, Kazuo, and Mariko and their stupid clicking cameras. I have to warn Jiro. Our plan won't work. If I want to claim Miyu's life for my own, if I'm going to make it out of Kuramagi with Jiro, then we can't follow the same path that led them to this—this double suicide, to avoid whatever horrible life kept them apart—

"Reiko? Hey! Hey, where the hell are you going?" Aki shouts. She's in full-on viper mode, spitting venom as she clatters after me in her wooden *geta*. "Don't you dare walk away from me! How dare you ruin my photo shoot!"

"I don't have time to explain." My voice feels like it doesn't come from me. It's guttural and rancid with rage. Am I speaking Japanese? I don't care anymore. Nothing matters but getting back to the stone. I have to warn Jiro that our plan won't work—that we need a new one. Whatever he and Miyu tried in the past—we can't let it come to that.

"What the hell?!"

Aki catches me by the baggy sleeve of my kimono and tries to yank me back into her. I swing around. Her eyes are narrowed daggers and her nails are vicious claws as she wraps both hands around my arm.

"This is my big day," Aki says, in a voice as thin as garrote wire. "Your crazy ass is *not* going to ruin this for me. I need you at the festival. Doing your job."

She tugs me forward, but she's expecting me to resist. Instead, I let her pull, then swing around her, toppling her over. She lets go to catch herself, but she's too late and crumples against the stones. Her shriek cuts off abruptly.

"I deserve this," I say, clearly now. I sound fierce. I feel unstoppable. Darkness creeps around my vision; the buzzing builds and builds. I am vengeance. I am the earthquake, consuming everything in my path, unleashing rivers of molten blood.

Akiko raises her head. A nasty gash crosses her forehead from her fall, already bubbling with red. "I'll kill you," she whispers. "You'll pay for this."

But I no longer have time for her. She is beneath my notice. She'll pay in due time.

For now, I have to warn Jiro.

A dull drumbeat carries me along the path, racing, racing, tumbling up steps, shoving my way through the thick crowds of tourists, though many of them dart out of my way as soon as they see me barreling along. *We can do this*, I hear, inside my head, and I smile. *We can have our revenge and keep Jiro safe. We can set things right.*

Yes. That's what I'm doing. I'm going to prevent a tragedy. I'll help Miyu—help *me*—find a way to be with Jiro. They needn't kill themselves. We deserve to succeed.

I fly up the *ryokan* staircase and rush into the room. Where's the stone? Where'd it go? I rip the sheets off of my pallet. Oh, God. Someone's already made up the room. What if they took it away? But no, there it is, lurking under the foot of the pallet. It's safe. Relief lurches through me, so powerful I could almost vomit. I tumble into bed as I clench the stone tight. *Yes. We can succeed.* It's the last thing I hear before the past envelops me.

❖

The festival is in full swing. Children with streamers and garlands of late-blooming flowers parade down the street; the echo of drums ricochets through the town. I am walking at Tsurube's side, displayed like a second-place prize. He struts beside me, but his gaze snaps franticly all around, darting down the gaps at the nape of every young woman's neck. I want to strangle him with his own *obi*.

"I'd forgotten what an embarrassment this little village is," Tsurube says, then clucks his tongue. "Kyoto is far better, as you'll learn. The beautiful riverwalk, the shrines, the geisha houses in the Gion District—not that you'll be enjoying those." He permits himself a self-satisfied grin. "You'll mostly be confined to the palace complex, of course, but I'm sure you'll enjoy yourself with the other wives. They're quite industrious with their needlework."

I smile so sharply at him I half hope he'll cut himself on it.

"I do hope you're still fertile," he adds, fingers spidering in the air. Protective. "Your father did make certain . . . assurances." Tsurube turns toward me, staring at me with those beady bird eyes. "How much of the poison did you *actually* drink?"

Poison? I blink, fighting down the sudden urge to strike him, though I'm not sure what he means. *Must wait, must wait, he'll get what he deserves soon*, my thoughts murmur. I ease my shoulders back. "Not enough, it would seem," I say.

He laughs, honking like a goose, drawing the stares of other villagers, but they look away as soon as he cuts his eyes toward them. "Oh, good, the sake house is still here. As good a place as any to pass the time until the festivities begin."

I spot Jiro on the other side of the square, browsing a merchant's stall that sells a collection of charms and offerings to the *kami*. I have to tell him—warn him *now* of the danger that awaits us. Something that will foil our plans, though I don't know what—something that made a love suicide our only way out. I look back at Tsurube, lowering my eyes like an obedient wife to be. "Oh, but my lord, I wish to purchase a charm. To wish us many children, you see."

His upper lip curls back as he considers. "Fine. But be quick about it." He gestures to the sake house. "I expect to find you waiting for me right outside of here."

Tied up like a horse at the hitching post. "Of course, my lord." I drop into as low a bow as I can manage, given the sickness swirling in my gut, then wait for him to enter the sake house.

I rush toward Jiro and brush past him, pausing only long enough to give him a significant glance. He nods, and I vanish around the corner, into a staircase that leads down to the next tier of streets.

Jiro rushes toward me, and we meet in the middle of the staircase. "Miyu." He grasps my arms. "I'm so glad I found you. I have good news."

Good news. "Jiro, listen to me. I'm afraid we're in grave danger—"

"No, Miyu, please. I spoke to Goemon, and—and there's a way for me to be free of my bond. I can leave the shogunate's service with no obligation, still receive my annual *koku*. All the money we'd need to live comfortably." He smiles so sweetly, so full of light.

Something in me tugs against my own instincts—a hesitation. Is it Miyu, sensing the danger that lays ahead on this path? But I want to avoid following her instincts. They led to her and Jiro's deaths. "How?" I ask. I have to proceed carefully. Find just the right turning point to prevent their fate.

Jiro glances over his shoulder, then looks back to me, gripping my hands tight. "I—All right. Please, what I'm about to tell you—we must keep it secret. We can do this, but I need your trust."

I nod, even as I feel my whole body tingle with chills.

"Goemon and I were sent here to investigate rumors of a plot. We'd been warned that the *daimyo* and his friends loyal to the emperor were planning to overthrow the shogun." Jiro trembles as he speaks; I realize he must be betraying a powerful vow to even share this knowledge with me. "So far we've found no evidence of this coup, though . . ." He looks down, cheeks darkening. "I, ah, confess I haven't been looking very hard, as I've been a bit . . . preoccupied."

I blush, too, and run my thumbs over his knuckles.

"But if I find evidence of such a plan . . . If there's anything you can tell me at all . . . It would be extremely valuable. That kind of information I could easily use to purchase my freedom. I would turn the information over to Goemon, and he'd take care of the rest. You and I could leave today, before that awful toad has a chance to miss you."

Miyu's body is in turmoil; her instincts screaming to turn and run. Fear prickles at the back of my neck; my heart pounds in time with the distant drums. But no. This is my chance. I can rewrite history for Miyu and Jiro. What if Miyu's instinct is to keep Father's secret, and that's the thing that ultimately drives her and Jiro to suicide after forces conspire to keep them apart in this life?

I have to tell him. I deserve this.

Even if Miyu hadn't.

"Yes." I let out my breath. "It's true. My father and the *daimyo* are involved. They're plotting some sort of ambush during the festival ceremony." I swallow; my throat is closing up on my words, but I have to go on. "I'm supposed to cause some sort of distraction, and then they'll ambush someone on the—the high mountain pass."

Jiro lowers our hands; he suddenly looks overcome with exhaustion, his face sagging, his shoulders slumped. "It's true, then."

"I'm afraid so. I don't know who they're attacking, but—"

Jiro flinches. "The shogun."

My eyes widen.

"He is arriving for the festival to announce the latest

216

decree regarding the barbarians at our gates. No one in Kuramagi was supposed to be aware of it, but . . . clearly that is not the case." He forces himself to smile. "But now we can prevent it. And I can buy my freedom—and yours, too."

I nod. I am still tingling all over, but maybe it is just residual. Relief. I am going to set things right—prevent whatever fate has befallen the lovers. Oh, God. An eager rush tingles all over my skin. This was going to be my life. Running away with Jiro. I am finally going to be free.

"Go—quickly. Go back to the *honjin* and gather your things. I'll report to Goemon now, then I need you to meet me in one hour."

"Where?" I ask. I'm already mentally inventorying Miyu's room. Beyond a few kimonos and her coat, I can't think of much else I need.

"Down the trail at the bottom of the village." Jiro squeezes my hands, then turns to climb the stairs. "We'll meet at the lovers' shrine."

By the time it dawns on me, he's already been swallowed up by the crowd.

How could the shrine already exist if Miyu and Jiro are still alive?

But—but if the lovers' shrine doesn't memorialize Miyu's and Jiro's love—what happened to them?

CHAPTER EIGHTEEN

I HAVE TO GET TO THE MUSEUM AND FIND OUT WHAT really happened to Miyu and Jiro. I throw the stone out of Miyu's pocket and slam back into myself in the *ryokan*. I have to save them from themselves.

Bile rises in my throat. Have I just condemned them to their death by ignoring Miyu's warning signs? I race down the stairs of the inn and dive into the swarming streets of Kura-magi. The amplified cries of a folk singing group blanket the village from the central square. But I need answers from somewhere else. I fly up the stairs, up, higher, heading for the highest tier, for the *honjin*, for the one person who may be able to tell me what's happening.

Don't bother, the voice says, in the back of my thoughts. *It's time. Time to give them what they deserve.*

But I can't listen. I need to know. I need to save Miyu.

I need to save myself.

❖

"The museum is permanently closed to you," the historian snaps at me, as soon as I tumble in the door. "Get out. And take your boots with you."

But I storm up to her. She's got to be at least sixty, possibly seventy; her skin is still mostly smooth, but I bet her bones could snap open like Pixy Stix. "I'm not going anywhere. You're going to tell me the truth—the whole truth."

"I don't know what you're talking about." She reaches for the receiver on an old black telephone resting on her desk.

I lunge for her and smack the phone from her hand. "I need the truth about the family that used to live in the *honjin*, back during the shogunate's time!" My words sound wrapped in thorns. I feel strong, like all the hate I've carved into my muscles is roaring to life. God, it feels great.

The woman's fearful expression eases, and she starts to laugh. "Ahhhh. I see. You want to know about the lovers' shrine."

"So it does have something to do with her family."

"Yes."

I'm looming over her still. "Tell me. The *truth* this time."

"Oh, it's such a tragic tale." She crosses her arms in front of her, a strange grin on her thinning lips. "The tale of Fumiko and the blacksmith. Yes, this is what you want to hear."

But I haven't heard either of those names before—not in this world or in Miyu's. "I don't understand."

"Fumiko was the eldest daughter of the man who ran the *honjin*, a loyal servant of the *daimyo*. Fumiko was married to the village blacksmith, you see, and she loved him very much.

"But the blacksmith fell in love with Fumiko's younger sister. They had a passionate tryst—everyone in the village knew. It was very disgraceful. The father threatened to kill the blacksmith if he did not end it with his youngest girl. He needed heirs—legitimate heirs, to serve the *daimyo*."

My legs wobble beneath me. Suddenly I have an awful, sick feeling about where this tale might lead.

"So the blacksmith and the younger sister made a suicide pact. They would die together, and be reunited in the next life."

"No," I say. This isn't making sense. "That's what the shrine says. But—but this isn't what happened. Miyu's still—she lived."

A distant laugh rolls through me—coming from me, though

I find nothing funny about this situation. My head buzzes. What's happening to me?

"Don't ever say that name," the historian screeches.

I charge her again, moving without thinking. I can't control myself. My hatred is a living thing, pulling all my strings. "Don't tell me what I can do." I have her by the throat; my spit freckles her face. "No one can tell me what I can and cannot do ever again."

I don't know where the words come from, but I know they are true. I didn't want my parents telling me who to love, how to act, what to study. I didn't want Hideki lording over me ever again. And I can't bear remembering Chloe telling me we were through. Why does she get to decide? Why shouldn't I have a say?

My life. My rules. Everyone else will get what they deserve.

"The truth." I tighten my grip. "All of it. *Now.*"

Finally she's showing some fear. She doesn't try to fight me off. "Fine! Fine! Just let me explain." She's trembling in my grasp. "The younger sister—that demon—she doesn't drink the poison. The blacksmith dies, but she lives. Then she goes to her sister, Fumiko, and tells her—'Now, we are even.'"

"So she seduced her sister's husband just to get him to kill himself?" I ask. "Why?"

But I already know why. Because I have the same blackness roiling in me like hot tar.

"For years of torment from an older sibling, I suppose."
The historian manages a weak shrug. "For a lifetime of cruelty. How can you explain a monster like her?"

"Leave Miyu out of this," I snarl. "She did what she had to do to survive." A sibling's cruelty—the worst kind. They're supposed to be your flesh and blood, your ally against all else. Who can blame Miyu for what she did? Who can blame me for wanting to leave a hateful mark of my own?

I am Miyu. Blackness warms my vision, then the words echo, louder, slicing up my thoughts. *I AM MIYU.*

The historian only scowls at me. "Her sister kills herself, because what kind of life can a widow have in those days? A terrible one. Better off just to die. Everyone made it out like a tragic lover's tale, when really, it was all about revenge."

Yes. Revenge. The word is a sweet sip of cool water. It is the earliest spring bloom. Revenge is all that matters. Revenge is what I deserve.

The historian shakes her head. "It was a great *haji*—a great shame. A disgrace. She was so hateful, that Miyu, and everyone knew it. But we tell the other story to try to keep Miyu away. She was so convinced the world had done her a great disservice . . . But then, when the samurai came . . ."

"Then what?" I renew my grip on her. "What about the samurai?"

She clucks her tongue. "Now, now, now. You're a hateful

girl, too, aren't you? Yes . . . It's no wonder she found you. You two are kindred souls."

Her words eat at me like acid. Kindred souls? What does she mean? I feel myself deflating. The humming fades; my limbs are fuzzy. I'm losing my grip on the historian—on my thoughts—on everything—

"Yes, Miyu, I know it's you. You can never hide from us for long."

My body is tensing up, coiled to strike. What is she talking about? How does she know? I try to speak, but can't fight past this hatred that burns like poison in my throat.

The historian is everywhere, her voice booming off the walls. The walls I've wiped and wiped and wiped again, for decades. Forever. I'm stuck here forever. "I'm sorry, Miyu. As surely as you try to get your vengeance, we'll always be ready to contain you."

I crumple to the ground. Dark cedar rafters spin and swirl around me; I think I'm throwing up. I fling one hand out and away from me, trying to swat away—something. Everything. The dark shadow always at my back is creeping forward, catching me off guard at last.

"Yes, Miyu, we've got you now. We'll stop you the same way we always have." Her voice turns bladed. "Perhaps this time, we can stop you for good."

I'm being dragged along the floor. A click. And then black.

I kick in the direction I think is the door, not that I can tell anything in the tarry black of the closet or whatever the hell she's locked me inside. I hear the slow, uncertain sounds of the older woman punching a telephone number into her phone. "Onagi-san," she says in Japanese. "I am afraid we have another one."

Another one? Another what? I pound again on the door, but she ignores me as she listens to whatever Mr. Onagi is saying in response.

"*Hai.* We must deal with her the same as all the rest. Bring her to the festival once you've gathered the others."

"Let me out!" I scream. What does she mean, "deal with me"? "You can't do this to us!"

Us. The word curls around me like a cat, rubbing up against me, marking its property. Miyu and me.

Yes. We are one and the same. You are so like me—and you will be me. I'll swap my life for yours.

Oh, God. Oh God oh God oh God, I wasn't imagining the voices, the dreams, the strange thoughts buzzing like wasps inside my head—

Don't you want revenge? she asks, that purring, rubbing feeling accompanying her words. *Don't you want to get what you deserve?*

I'm shaking as I huddle in the thin cheap kimono Aki swaddled me in. I'm trying to hold onto myself. But where do I end, and where does Miyu begin? I walked the path of hatred long before I found her stupid stone. I perfected that path. She just gave me a new way to channel it.

You see, Reiko? We're one and the same. You should be me. And I can be you.

Is she right? What do I have to live for, really? Not my brother or my parents. Not Chloe. Not Kenji, shoving me away. It's true that like her I want revenge. I want to give Aki what she deserves. But this throbbing, growing seed of hatred inside me—that's not me, it's got to be her—

She laughs inside of me. *I wouldn't be so sure.*

My dreams flood my thoughts—glimpses of the earth bucking around me, of the rivers of blood. No. Those are Miyu's. But the way I respond to them . . . the way I feel an itch inside me, wanting them as badly as the first time I glimpsed them . . .

Yes. We are one and the same. What's the use in fighting it? I was every bit as hateful a fiend as Miyu long before I came to Kuramagi. And I know it, deep down. I know the things I've done for revenge. The way I pushed Hideki. The real reason Chloe spread my photos around the school. The disaster I've set at the cultural festival. I know the things I've done. Period.

I have to keep Miyu safe. No one else understands her like I do.

When the samurai came—that's what the historian said. *When the samurai came . . .* What happened then? I dig through the layers of the kimono and find the sagging pocket of the inner robe where I tucked the stone. If I can't help myself here, now, then I can help Miyu back then.

Yes. You understand. We can help each other, she says. *You can help me, and I won't let them do to you what they mean to do.*

I will. I'll keep us both safe.

❖

I am still in the village streets, not long after Jiro left to make his exchange. His information for his life. I am down a level from the main square, but I can hear the crowds from here—the chanting, the shouts, punching like fists. The festival is in full swing.

But something has shifted. Thick clouds, dark as smoke, hang low overhead. The air smells metallic. And the shouts— they are no longer cries of joy. No more folk songs twist and braid through the crowd. All I hear are ugly, brutal words, battering against a single subject. Has my father's plan begun? Or has Jiro managed to stop them?

Danger, Miyu whispers, either to herself or to me—it doesn't matter which. Yes. I have to agree with her. There is danger in the air, and whenever there is danger, the villagers turn on us.

Just like they did when we laid our sister to rest.

But they got what they deserved, we reminded ourselves. Our sister and her husband both. A childhood of her taunts, her greed, her gossip about us. At long last, we'd repaid our debt to her.

Now there are other debts to repay.

I need to get back to the *honjin* to pack. I'm not sure how much time has passed, but I know I have to meet Jiro at the shrine soon. I charge up the narrow stairwell and turn down the main street, away from the square. But the wall of people pushes me back; I stumble into their flow and can't swim to shore. As soon as I turn to face the square, I see why.

Goemon paces the length of the dais at the heart of the square. Lined up before him, resting on their knees, hands bound behind their backs, sit all of the *daimyo*'s conspirators in a row. Yodo and my father. The *daimyo* himself. The rotund man and the spidery one. Only Tsurube stands unbound—I have no doubt he was only too happy to change his allegiance at the first hint of a threat to his way of life.

And then, at the end of the row, a vicious grin slicing across his face, is Jiro.

I draw a ragged breath. He looks so pleased with foiling my father's plan that he frightens me. But he must play the part of the triumphant warrior even if it was his final act as a samurai. As soon as his duty is done, he and I will be free.

". . . for crimes against the shogunate. But it is not only

those you see here before you who are guilty. It is each and every one of you who allowed such a crime to fester in your midst," Goemon says.

Jiro nods, topknot bobbing as he does. "As far as I'm concerned, every last person of Kuramagi should lose their heads. The way they should have been dealt with in Mito and Chōshū."

There is something vulgar in Jiro's expression. He looks so pleased with himself, so delighted to hold his *katana* free of its sheathe. But then, he always did want to make use of his sword.

And now it seems he's engineered for himself the perfect chance.

And suddenly I know. This isn't his last moment of acting before his obligations to the shogunate are finished.

This is the first time he's not acting at all.

He never wanted us, Miyu insists.

No. He never wanted us. We were only ever a tool for him, something he used to lever himself into ever higher regard in the shogunate's esteem. He was never going to run away with me. He saw me as a coward, a desperate little girl he could use. Someone so desperate for love she would tell him whatever he needs to know.

We have to get away. The urgency thrums through me, louder even than the drums. If we don't leave now, we'll be up on that platform, too. It will be our throat pressed against the folded steel, our entrails waiting to spill across the stage—

But then Jiro turns. Those hateful coal-black eyes meet ours across the crowd. The darkness on his face swells up like a bruise.

Run, Miyu. Run!

I shove my way toward the back of the square, elbows swinging wildly, sandals clattering across the cobblestones. The smell of incense and sake burn at my throat as I shove toward the edge of the crowd and break out into a run. The stables. I can make it to the stables, the ones near the *honjin*, as long as the crowd slows Jiro down as much as it had slowed me. The *daimyo* keeps a whole fleet of horses at the ready, and his estate is only a little farther up the road, at the far end of this street, behind our home.

Shouting swirls behind me, crackling like dead leaves. But I can't stop to make sense of it. I have to run.

My lungs feel heavy as lead by the time I reach the top of the road and clamber over the retaining wall that surrounds the *daimyo*'s estate. My wooden sandals fall off as I swing up and over. Don't bother with them; there's no time. I'll ride barefoot and naked if that's what it takes. I have to flee. I curve around the estate and find the stables by their smell. I pick the fastest-looking horse I can find—not too big, not too old, one with restless limbs that happily snuffles at my hand as I hold it out. It'll have to do. I don't have the first clue about how to saddle a horse, but the saddle hanging on the side of his pen seems about the right size.

We must move quickly. It's already happening. It's already too late.

I squeeze my eyes shut and see once more: the whoosh of steel through cold air; the rivers of blood—

Okay. I have to focus. Hideki and I went horseback riding once with our parents; surely it'll come back to me like riding a bike. I sling the saddle over his back, then step around to his side to buckle the saddle underneath, taking care never to cross behind his rear—

A shadow spins toward me from the doorway of the stables. I freeze; holding still against the retaining wall that separates the horse's pen from his neighbor's. Please, oh, please, stupid horse, don't give me away.

"Miyu? Oh, Miyu, my darling Miyu-chan." Jiro's voice sounds dipped in poison. "I know you don't want to do anything rash. Not when we have our *whole future* ahead . . ."

My rage is hot as phosphorous, burning a hole through my chest. Liar. Traitor. He used me like everyone else. Dumped on me simply because he could, because I was there, because everyone knew I'd take it. But he has underestimated the strength of my hate.

"Don't be rash, Miyu. You don't want to make a fool of yourself. I'd hate to see you suffer any more than you must."

Rash? He dares to call me rash? Fool. Miyu and I have played the long game of vengeance. A smile unfurls on my face, snapping into place like a sail. Just ask my sister and her husband. I laughed in spite of myself. The dark haze I've felt hanging over me for far too long settles, and I wear it like a mantle. I'll always have my revenge.

Always.

Always, Miyu sighs, her relief echoing my own.

A blade punches through the thin panel that separates this stall from the next, inches from where my arm was pressed. I roll away as it slices its way down and retracts.

No. He will not stop me.

I grab the nearby rake. My anger is a cleansing fire, giving me focus. I will survive. I brace myself and wait until Jiro's face appears in the doorway, teeth bared, eyes wild.

His frame fills the exit and I jab the rake at him—

But his sword arm is faster, honed from years of training. He slices away the rake end, then snatches the remaining pole and yanks me toward him. I topple forward, socked feet slipping easily on the damp hay, and barely catch myself from landing on my face.

I let go of the rake handle and swing my hands up in the air to surrender. But he doesn't stop his attack. He slams his body into me, pushing us against the far wooden wall of the stable, then holds his sword against my throat to pin me in place. The blade burns against my skin as he sneers.

"I have no more use for you. Your purpose has been served." He spits at me; the saliva dribbling down my raised forearm.

I should be shaking. Cowed, terrified. But no. We no longer have a space in our black hearts for fear, Miyu and I.

"How could you ever be so foolish to believe anyone would love you?" Jiro's look of contempt stokes my certainty as I slowly slip my hand into the bun of my hair. The vein of his neck dances with each cruel syllable. "You are nothing. Just another dishonorable whore."

The darkness flutters in me. We are so much more than that. Far more powerful than he realizes.

"Dishonor?" I laugh. "You say *I'm* the one without honor?"

I bring my knee up into his groin. He recovers quickly, his samurai reflexes kicking in, but in that split second, his grip on the sword loosens. That's when I strike. I swing my hand down, snatching the long pin holding up my bun. It gleams in the darkness as I drive it home, right into that dancing vein on his throat.

I can almost see it now, meticulously marked and labeled on Hideki's study guides back in his apartment. *Fig. 1. Jugular vein. If punctured, patient may experience severe blood loss.*

Hot red blood fountains from his throat, spraying across me as he screams. The heat is such a comfort on my face as he sinks to his knees. I will wear it, unlike the entrails the children threw at me on my first visit to the village, as a badge of honor.

Let red drip down my limbs. Let me paint my legacy across the earth as I walk.

Jiro's screams are sweeter than any chorus, as luscious as a symphony. He tries to swing the *katana* at me, but he is losing control, and fast. The sword clatters from his hand into the quickly muddying dirt.

Too quickly, his screams end; the pools of blood cease to flow.

I seize the *katana* from where it fell, the handle slippery. Then I rip the *wakizashi* from his belt. One weapon in each hand.

Why stop here? Miyu asks. *Why only him, when so many have done us harm?*

I feel my denial forming, calcifying like a pearl deep inside of me. I want to say that I got the revenge I needed; that my debts are paid. But I can't bring myself to argue. Every time I try, I feel the buzz, I hear Miyu's words circling in my head. I'm not in control of myself. I am only a passenger in Miyu's life. She has control.

Come, she tells me. *It's time for the rest of them to pay.*

CHAPTER NINETEEN

I MOVE WITHOUT THINKING, WITHOUT NEEDING TO control my own body. Maybe Miyu's in control of me now—I can't say for sure. But it doesn't matter. We are one mind, one will, and that is the will to wreak as much destruction as we possibly can. Jiro has paid the price for betraying us, but there are so many more who have yet to pay. I'm willing to give Miyu the power to make them pay. She deserves it.

The world shifts around me, past and present swirling together. I don't remember letting go of the stone. When did I? The village fades, and I'm plunged back into the darkness of the storage closet at the museum. Everything smells of metal, or maybe it's the memory of Jiro's blood, but then our hand closes around a splintering wooden handle. We feel up the handle to some manner of rusted, ancient farm implement. Yes. This is what we need.

We start hacking at the door. The thin boards crack and rip apart easily, fine as fish bones. Within minutes, we're able to reach out of the deep gash and unlatch the door from the exterior.

Yes. It's time. Time to have our revenge. We're going to make all of them pay for what they've done. Miyu's voice is breathless, raspy as a saw in my mind. *All our lives, we've suffered, but it's finally time to make it right.*

All my life. I look down at the farm tool in my hand, some sort of gardening trowel. Hardly menacing. Maybe not bad for hacking down doors, but it's so dull and rusted, I can't imagine it being any use for what Miyu wants. (What I want? Yes. What *I* want.)

Upstairs, she urges me. I don't even make the conscious choice to go—my feet move of their own volition, or maybe she's guiding me. The world flickers around us: light and dark, the possessions of Miyu's family warping in and out. We are both dressed in kimonos, but the colors shift, my body shifts—she's a few inches shorter than me—but we are all the same, we are all one machine of pure vengeance with a samurai's blood splattered hot across our face.

We are one and we will kill.

Upstairs. A sword on display. I seize it and set off for the main road toward the festival.

There are still so many debts left to repay.

Miyu's thoughts chatter inside me like a screeching flock of crows. *For years, I suffered my sister's torment. She earned her suffering. I bought and paid for her death with my own life, with all the lies she spread about me as a child, the men she chased from me, with her own failures that she told Father had been my own.*

Why should she take a husband first, a respected member of the village? Mind you, he was a dreadful man, an utter bore and a drunk and, quite obviously, a lecher, but what man isn't? All my suffering was worth it the day they put her in the ground next to him. The "lovers' shrine" was but another hateful lie, another attempt to best me. The villagers of Kuramagi excel at concealing the ugliness beneath their façades. But I'll have my revenge for that, too.

Shadows swirl at our feet as we march down the winding cobblestone path away from the *honjin*. The amplified thud of pop ballad wars with the executioner's drumbeat as we walk; a rotten-smelling wind rakes through our cheap kimono in one time and our bloodied hair in another. We are vengeance and we are hate. People scamper from our path, hands clenched over their mouths to smother out their gasps. Whether they wear vinyl dresses or soft cotton robes, their reactions are the same.

Run. Run from the monsters you've forged with your cruelty, your vendettas pushed too far, your determination to have the last word. Run, before we return it a thousandfold.

My sword arm itches—how Miyu aches to lash out at nearly everyone we pass! I dream of it, of the blood splattering us anew, warm as baptismal water ready to wash away our sins. Is it my instinct and restraint that keeps us from striking them? I wish I could say so, but I want to lash out as badly as Miyu does. I want to make my artwork real. To paint my photographs with red.

How I wish Chloe were here, to see how I've fulfilled the prophecy of the artwork that she urged me to make. For I've done this all before, haven't I? I have walked this path of hatred with darkness throbbing in my heart.

Chloe remembers. I remember. I'm practically delirious now with the memory of it, the way I got my revenge. On that dark fall day, when I found Chloe in Portland in another girl's arms, I didn't rush back home. No.

I waited, a plan forming in my mind with frightful calm.

I waited for her new girlfriend to leave the house where they were couch-surfing. Chloe apparently made good on her promise to run away from home. I watched until Chloe left for work, and Selena went downtown, to some all-ages punk rock show. Selena. My prey. I zipped up my hoodie and followed her into the club.

God, how she bored me. Chain smoking clove cigarettes

with gauge-eared girls and boys made of twigs. Sneaking swigs from her friends' flasks and talking too loudly with her empty, pointless words. What could Chloe possibly see in her? How could she have replaced me with this loser? I went to the alleyway to wait.

And then she came out of the club alone, eyes wet, cigarette limp in her mouth. She didn't see me—her back was to me as she muttered to herself and smoked. I was crouched behind a dumpster, surrounded by cast-off bottles. Almost without thinking, I seized one by the neck, warm beer sloshing down my wrist as I charged at her. In that moment, I didn't care about the consequences. All that mattered was the way it felt to swing the bottle up into her jaw, the way it shattered apart, spraying us both with beer and green glass.

It felt amazing. It felt like freedom, like I'd never even known.

Yes. I love revenge as much as Miyu. I want that feeling of freedom again. Alone as Reiko, I thought I had freed myself when I made a bloody mess of Selena's chin. But even though no one saw me and I made it back to Berkeley, Chloe knew. **I KNOW IT WAS YOU**, her first email read, and a half dozen more followed. **I CAN'T PROVE IT, BUT I KNOW IT. YOU NEED HELP.**

I deleted them all.

Weeks passed. My decision from RISD came—wait-listed. And then one Sunday night, a single email made it through my email block: **YOU ARE ONE SICK, TWISTED, VIOLENT INDIVIDUAL AND YOU WILL ONLY GET WORSE. YOU NEED HELP. AND I'M GOING TO MAKE SURE YOU GET IT.**

That was the night before my paintings showed up at school, and the rest was a blur of benzos and small groups and waxed linoleum floors.

I deserve freedom. I deserve revenge. That night in the alley, I thought I'd paid Chloe back for leaving me by slicing open her new girlfriend's chin. But then she got me sent to the psych ward. Had I made those paintings? Yes. Was I violent? Certainly. But she'd made me that way. Couldn't she see? She'd *made* me that way. Miyu understood that. Miyu would have done the same.

I can smell the pyres of the village square now—the incense and stew and sake set out for all of Kuramagi to enjoy as they prepare for the annual purification ceremony. Only today would serve a different purpose. The square is a sea of kimonos and soldiers with their swords. Heads start to turn toward us as we near the square; men start to whisper and point. A soldier grips his sword hilt tight and takes a step our way.

No. We cannot be stopped. We've earned our revenge.

Once you are branded a whore, then a whore you become. Father had to keep up a good front for the daimyo, *but he'd gladly sell me out to those willing to pay a high enough price. They told me purity was a virtue, but it seems it's not as much a virtue as a fat purse. Jiro was the first man I chose for myself, after my sister's husband, and look where that landed me.*

The world warps around us—fleeting images of the kind that had haunted my dreams flash before my eyes. The leering herb merchant with his belly slit open and his innards flopping limply from the wound. The children, all the children, face down in pools of blood. Even the samurai took grievous wounds, before they cut Miyu down.

And suddenly I understand. Miyu had done all of this. She'd slaughtered Kuramagi in her life, and now she wants me to slaughter it in mine.

You deserve this freedom, Reiko, she hisses, words whipping at me like a gale. *You deserve to make them pay.*

I think of Hideki. The good child, our parents' golden boy. Winner of scholarships, charmer of dinner guests, proof of their success. "They should have stopped with me," he once said, right before he cut my ponytail off with garden shears. He deserves to pay most of all.

I surge forward, buoyed by Miyu's words buzzing in my head, only to stumble on the uneven stones.

But then I remember how he let me come visit him in Berkeley after graduation, when I was unable to stand another moment around our parents. Hideki and I may never have been friends, but we both understood the kind of purgatory that was House Azumi, no questions asked. He looked so old, so exhausted, that weekend; thick bags bunched the once smooth skin under his eyes and his hair hung forward in oily clumps. His decision was weighing on him, I knew. He was going to quit med school, though our parents would cut him off when they found out.

That afternoon, while I was laying in a puddle of misery on the couch thinking about Chloe, Hideki came and sat beside me. Instinctively I touched the five bruises on my wrist. How long had it been since he'd last hurt me there? How long had I been doing it to myself?

"Listen, kiddo, I'm only going to say this once to you." Hideki pushed the hair out of his face. "I've been a real shit brother, all right? I know that. I've done horrible things to you. Made your life hell sometimes. And Mom and Dad— well, they're more inclined to like someone like me, who gets into med school and kisses ass and all that. Even when I was young I knew that, and I took advantage of it."

He shifted on the couch. "But I love you. You're different, okay. You're weird as hell, but you're true to yourself. You don't have to play Mom and Dad's little accomplishments game, because you've figured out how to succeed outside of their rules. You're going to art school, for God's sake. You'll be among kindred souls. That's *incredible*. Do you have any idea how envious I am of you for that? If I could, I'd . . . God. I don't even know what I'd do. It's hard enough just having to hide this one tiny little part of my life from them, and I . . ."

He shook his head. "I don't know. I guess all I'm saying is, cheer the fuck up."

The memory still feels gentle, even though the rage boils inside me. Hideki had never been so kind to me. Not without a hammer waiting just behind the velvet. How dare he tell me to *cheer up*? When it was years of his lies, his bruises, his manipulation that led me to Chloe in the first place. And now he had revealed his one vulnerability. I had a way to make him pay.

It only took one email, one cell phone snapshot of his withdrawal letter, to tear his whole world down.

"I told Mom and Dad," I said, before he could even set down his keys after returning from his final exam. "They know."

He was already shaking. "Know what?" he asked, the hairline fractures in his tone belying his attempts at calm.

"That you're not going to go to med school after all. They know all about your honorable discharge, about Marco, about everything."

Hideki was shaking. Our parents knowing that he was discharged from the military because a bunch of homophobes beat him up and that he was backpedaling from his med school plans—that would cause them to renounce him utterly. Financially. Emotionally. Completely cut off.

And that was the one thing that Hideki could not take.

Without their money and approval he would be a worthless nobody, just like me.

"You're lying," he said.

I shrugged. "You can ask them yourself."

He grabbed me by the throat. "Liar. You're a fucking liar." His hand shook as he squeezed. "You didn't. Admit it, you wouldn't do that. I'll—I'll tell them about your ex-girlfriend— I'll tell them everything—"

"What do I care?" I asked. "I've got nothing to lose."

"They can't own me." His gaze narrowed. "You can't own me. No one can."

"You keep telling yourself that."

I locked the door to my guest bedroom and slept wonderfully. At long last, I was not the problem child. But when I got up in the night to use the restroom, I found him with potassium cyanide—homemade; he knew his organic chemistry—trying to burn a hole through his trachea.

Isn't it wonderful, revenge? Miyu asks. The crowds part for us as we approach the square. *Retribution will set you free. Your tormentors deserve it, as do mine.*

I want to agree—to feel the sword plunge into resistant flesh, to see the look on Akiko's face when I put an end to her selfish cruelty once and for all. But when I try to picture it, all I see is Hideki, plugged with all those tubes. I feel his hand around my wrist once more. He tried to speak to me, but the plastic down his throat made it impossible (to say nothing of the partial hole there). So he wrote it down.

We've always been two snakes, biting each other's tails. Isn't it time we called a truce?

Truce. Hah. I'm just as angry now as I was then. But the image nags at me; I hadn't stopped, at the time, to wonder what he meant. Biting each other's tails—no beginning or end. No knowledge of who started it. No way to make it end without destroying us both.

My arm starts to sag; the sword is so heavy. I guess I've always known we would destroy ourselves. I guess this is the natural path toward our destruction.

We must vanquish our tormentors. My fellow villagers and the samurai who betrayed me. Your friends and family.

Yes, I think, with an eager sigh. Yes. She's right—of course she is. Why did I question it? The perfect end to our journey.

And you, Reiko . . . my cruelest tormentor of all.

I hesitate. What does she mean? I thought we were a team. I try to slow down, but my muscles are no longer my own. Miyu keeps us moving forward.

You didn't think you were blameless in this, did you? Her laughter scrapes through me like a rusted spoon. *Yes, Reiko. Of course you're at fault. You found my* magatama *in the woods— the home of my spirit. You thought you could claim my life without consequence.*

But—but she wanted me to find her. Didn't she? That's

why I'm here. United by our rage. Destined to seek vengeance together. My stomach twists. Miyu's my kindred spirit, helping me achieve what I've only dreamed about. We're meant to do this together. Aren't we?

Oh, we are. But one of us must be destroyed by our act of vengeance.

Miyu laughs.

And it's certainly not going to be me.

I try to let go of the sword, but my fingers are locked into place around its grip. No. I'm supposed to be in charge, getting my revenge. (Is it revenge? Or am I the one who started it?) I want to scream, but my throat has melted away; my jaw is caked in blood. We are two snakes, biting each other's tails. Where does one payback end and another begin?

It ends here, with me trapped inside Miyu—or her trapped inside me—and I'm helpless to watch as she makes her way toward the festival stage, sword blade glinting in the afternoon light.

CHAPTER TWENTY

ONE OF THE FESTIVAL WORKERS CHASES AFTER US, clattering along in her wooden sandals. "Miss, please come back here. You are not permitted into the crowd with any decorative weapons! Miss! Miss!" But there's no stopping us. She is a spirit of vengeance and I am her vessel. The woman snags me by the dangling sleeves of my kimono, but Miyu shoves her off of us easily, snarling, raising the sword in warning.

Franco's number is winding down on stage—Akiko is next, starting with a joint duet. Miyu's going to use me to kill her. Kill as many people as I can. I thought it's what I wanted, too. Revenge. But she's right about one thing—revenge is a cycle, and it's impossible to know where it begins. Now I'm helpless to watch as Miyu continues our own circle of violence. I wanted this. Oh, God, I let this happen.

Distantly, I hear the shuffle and shout of the historian from the *honjin* and of Mr. Onagi. "Stop her! Miyu is back!"

I try to scream, but my own throat shuts me down. My hands betray me, clammy and sure on the sword's hilt. Whatever they're shouting now is lost in the rainstorm of applause for Franco as his number concludes. All I can do is watch.

No. Wait.

The moment I stop trying to fight Miyu, to take control of my body, the streets twist and the light shifts. It's like I've varnished away a painting to find an older version hidden underneath. The colors of everyone's clothing are softer, and the buildings, fresher. The tang of horse manure lurks beneath the heady mix of sake and fish stew.

When I let go of the struggle, I fall back into Miyu's life.

I relax—and Miyu's father and his co-conspirators are lined up on the dais before me.

I test my hand—and find it obeying me. I drum my fingers forward, then backward against the *katana*'s hilt. Yes. Miyu may have control of my body, but I can control hers.

If I can't stop her in my world, then maybe I can in hers.

Soldiers in tightly woven vests of plated armor surge through the crowd toward me; heads whip my way as everyone begins to talk at once. I only catch snippets, but they're enough to spark my anger again—*whore, liar, thief, ingrate*. Let them hate me. Let them think what they will. Whether Miyu deserves it or not, it matters little to me.

Yes, Miyu: I don't care anymore about your suffering.

The soldiers reach for me, but I keep my chin high and meet Goemon's gaze. He's scrutinizing me with those slimy lizard eyes of his, pursing his thick froggish lips noticing Jiro's blood, still slick and not on my kimonu. Then he nods, ever so slightly, and lifts his hand.

"Stand down," he calls. The soldiers cease, only feet away from me. "Let us hear what the wench has to say for herself."

I close my eyes, briefly, just long enough to glimpse Miyu's memories. I know how this scene played out for her: the rivers of blood. The wink of the sword as it slashed through the village, striking again and again. Tears mingling with red on her cheeks, sizzling against her hatred-hot skin. She carved through them indiscriminately, through children and women and men, and plunged her sword into her father's chest.

"All of you must pay," she whispered through clenched teeth. "The shogunate. The *daimyo*. My family. Everyone is to blame."

She killed as many as she could before the samurai brought her down.

I won't let her do it again.

Jiro's *katana* clanks against the cobblestones as I let it slip from my hand.

"What has become of our affirmations, the ones we swear before the *kami*?" I gesture toward Miyu's father; he tugs against the soldier's firm grip on his shoulder. "You have not honored me as a family member should. You never loved me. I've only been a burden in your mind—you blame me for my mother's death. You let your resentment of me fester like scum in a stagnant pond."

The buzzing builds inside of me—Miyu is checking in. *Stop it! Silence, you fool!* she cries. *Pick up your sword and give them what we deserve!*

But as she chastises me, I can see a glimpse of my world. So long as I distract her here, she can do nothing there.

"The rest of you have shown me nothing but cruelty, and I have done my damnedest to repay you in kind. There is no reverence in Kuramagi, no respect for our fellow person. We show no honor here. No virtue."

But they made it that way, Miyu whines. *It's their doing. I was only returning the suffering they brought upon me!*

"And you, samurai, alleged servants of the shogun—what of your code? What would the samurai of old think of your ways?" I snort. "You resent your station—errand boys for a clueless, ill-prepared young shogun who you freely acknowledge doesn't deserve his post. You serve the shogun only when it suits you. You lie and you cheat."

"Mind your tongue," Goemon shouts, but I mark how he takes a step back.

"Would I be justified in seeking revenge against you all? Perhaps. And perhaps you'd be justified in cutting me down in return."

I'm shaking now; the buzzing presses against my mind like a ravenous horde. Miyu's howls have turned wordless as she tries to force my hand. But I'm here now. This is for me to choose.

"My hatred is . . . a physical thing. I've made it manifest, calcified it, condensed it like a stone." I reach into my pocket. The stone is burning against my hand as I pull it out. "I wanted to make a weapon of it. A cursed instrument that would find revenge across the centuries."

NO! Miyu screams, a thousand voices echoing her own. *We must fight them! They have to pay!*

"But it must end somewhere." I raise the stone overhead with both hands. "I must have the courage to end it."

Once more, I glimpse into my world—I see Aki on stage, watching me with undisguised fear. But she is singing, struggling on as I climb the dais stairs. Back in Miyu's body, I climb those same stairs and place the stone upon the altar, keeping one finger pressed against its edge.

I lift one of the heavy gray altar stones and smash it against the black curved one as hard as I can.

The stone cracks into three main chunks and a dusting of others. Miyu's screams surge forth in a crackling black cloud, buzzing, swarming, spreading like wasps over the village square.

The villagers scream and throw their hands over their heads to shield themselves. But I bask in it. The useless hissing Miyu makes, fades away, eroding into nothingness.

As Miyu's presence dims, so too does the scene before me. The villagers' screams turn into Akiko's pounding pop song, shaking the planks beneath my feet; their robes transfigure into hunchbacked retirees in quilt jackets, or stiletto-wearing trendsetters, or slouchy salarymen looking ill at ease in their off-duty jeans. The smells are shot through with frying oil and diesel and sweat as everyone screams and writhes. I stand in the wings of the dais, still clutching the sword.

As the stage light I rigged begins to fall.

CHAPTER TWENTY-ONE

"MOVE!" I SCREAM. "GET OFF THE STAGE!"

Aki shoots a death glare my way, but Kenji charges forward and pushes her out of the way. The light crashes to the stage with a fearful crack. Sparks, fire, all the kindling I'd placed—

"The fire extinguishers," I shout. "Behind the drum kit."

Kenji and Mariko find the extinguishers and start to douse the blaze. People are shoving back from the stage, still startled, unsure if the pyrotechnics are part of the show. But they manage to tamp it out. Aki is unharmed. Pissed, but alive.

"What the fuck is wrong with you?"

Before I can answer, though, Mr. Onagi, the historian, and Sierra are surrounding me, seizing me by the shoulders and trying to pry my fingers from the sword hilt. "We are sorry, Miyu, but it is time for your fun to end. Lock her up. I'll make the call." The historian purses her lips. "She can't walk freely."

"Wait. I'm not Miyu," I cry. Not anymore. "I stopped her."

The historian's grasp on my arm starts to falter. "That isn't possible," she says.

Mr. Onagi nods, and they begin to haul me down the stairs. "I'm afraid we can't take your word."

"She's gone, I swear! It's me! It's over!"

Mr. Onagi loosens his grip on me, but his anger is pulsating as he speaks. "You found that monster's altar. You brought her back."

"You could have killed us all," the historian adds. "We can't let Miyu kill again."

"But I didn't kill you all. I stopped her. For good." I yank my arm free of her grip with a glower and dig in the pocket of my robe. "See?"

I produce the fractured chunks of the black stone. It's a medium shade of gray now, and cold to the touch; no buzzing. No whispers. No link to Miyu's world. Only a rock.

They look the rock over. "Her *magatama*," the historian whispers. "Where did you find this?"

"It was in the makeshift temple buried off of the path to the lovers' shrine. I think the earthquake exposed it again," I say.

The historian and Mr. Onagi exchange looks. "We'll have to verify it with the priests," he says.

The historian looks from the shattered rock toward me. "What did she do to you?"

"She . . . she wanted me to repeat the cycle." My voice falters.

I squeeze my eyes shut, trying to forget the way the buzzing felt, pulsing through my veins. I remember the feel of my dark and sickly heart. But I feel it no longer.

I'm free. Kuramagi is free.

❖

"I owe you an apology," I say to Kenji, over our dinner of *shabu-shabu* at the *ryokan*. Mr. Onagi was none too pleased serving me, but apparently he and the rest of the village's secret-keepers have decided to let the whole matter of Miyu drop, seeing as how I managed to destroy the stone so they will not be threatened by her again. So he can get the chopstick out of his ass.

"For what?" Kenji asks, turning his head toward me so the others can't hear.

"I came to Japan to work out my personal demons." Swish, swish goes my slice of raw beef in the hot broth. *Shabu-shabu.* "But I just ended up finding more."

Kenji's brow furrows. "You worked them out in the end, didn't you?"

I'd explained what happened to Kenji. I owed the truth to him, at least—but I'm not certain he believed me. "Yeah." I smile weakly. "I suppose I did."

Across the table Aki squeals, clutching her phone. "Suzuki wants me to do a photo shoot with her!" She has her arms around Tadashi's neck. "Reiko, you let me down today, but I'm sure you can make it up to me."

I smirk. "I'm so glad you've picked a suitable punishment."

I'm expecting another epic rant from her, but she just smiles. "You're weird, Reiko. But it works for you. You know, it's kind of funny." One corner of her mouth twitches up. "All my life, it was Reiko this, Reiko that. I was always intimidated by you."

"What, me? Not Hideki?"

Akiko laughs. "My father has a lot more respect for the artistic types than your parents." I'm stunned, but she adds, "But now I just know you're weird." Kenji raises his eyebrows at me as he picks up the sake bottle and tops off everyone's glasses. My plate, I realize, is empty; it feels good to have the slightest hint of tightness in my belly from eating just enough food.

Sierra brings dessert around—green tea ice cream—and

offers me a scoop. "You doing okay?" she asks me in a low tone.

I turn my face toward hers. She's unafraid of me now. I no longer feel the buzz, the haze. I smile back at her, light as a breeze.

"I think I'm ready to go home," I say.

Back in Tokyo, I do a few more photo shoots for Akiko to earn the last bit of cash I need before returning to the States for the spring semester at RISD. Kenji and I spend our last few lunches together brainstorming on his comic book. "You really should try to get this published," I tell him. "Unless you want to keep drawing cartoon collies slurping ramen for the rest of your career."

He shrugs. "I'd love to go to art school, get some discipline. The Japanese style is really rigid, though. No one wants to feature characters like this—they don't fit the *manga* conventions."

"You could always go to RISD," I say with a grin.

"Right. Like I could afford that." His cheeks are turning a deep, bruised shade; he stares down into his sushi plate.

"There are plenty of scholarships. Probably some great ones for international students." I tilt my head as I flip through his sketchbook. "Or—or anywhere, really, in the States. Something to consider."

On the morning I leave, Akiko is supposed to accompany us to Narita Airport, but she and Tadashi get into a fight after she lands a spot on a Tokyo fashion program, and we never say a proper farewell. Live and let live, I suppose.

On the plane, waiting to take off, I finally open the email from Hideki. **Why did we do it, Reiko?** he asked me. **Why were we always at each other's throats?**

There was always some score to settle, I reply at last. **Revenge for revenge . . . the tally just kept climbing.**

His answer is waiting for me by the time we land.

Let's wipe it clean.

I reach for my own wrist, to press that painful chord against my skin. But then I stop. Let my hands hang limp. Time to break the cycle.

I head to RISD the very next week. At first, I'm angry that I don't get a single room in the dormitories, and they stick me with a snotty ceramist who looks down on all modern Asian styles as overly consumerist and imperial, but she ends up spending most her time at her boyfriend's apartment anyway, so I don't mind so much. I can lose myself in my design work—a seamless blend of photography, digital design, and illustration, when I can work with talented illustrators in class projects.

Hideki emails me every Friday morning, tells me how

physical therapy is going. I send a drawing back. I feel safer with him this way.

Sierra emails me toward the end of the spring semester to say she's coming back to Connecticut to visit her family for a few weeks, and would love to catch up, though both our lives are probably way more boring now. **Boring is good,** I tell her. And we set a date to meet for coffee.

I get another email, too, from an address I don't recognize. The attachments contain a series of illustrated comics panels. A bony slip of a girl, her face fierce, her feet planted, her chin lifted to stare ahead. Kenji's drawings—the character he based off of me.

Your background art is shit, I tell him, in my email back.

Yeah, I know. Still looking for the right illustrator to help me flesh it out. Job's yours if you want it.

And before I know it, I'm working on the comic with him, trading artwork across the sea featuring a character inspired by a girl who is no longer me. But I'm all right with it. I'm okay with becoming who I'm meant to be and leaving that girl behind. I'm okay with being me. And no one else.

THE END

AUTHOR'S NOTE

REIKO AND MIYU'S STORY CAME TO ME OUT OF NOTH-
ingness—a night of fog and drums.

My husband Jason and I went to Japan for our honeymoon in late 2014, and after an exhausting few months of
wedding preparation and deep, major edits to my third
book, *Dreamstrider*, all I wanted to do was relax in the hot
springs and eat some wonderful meals. "I know you too well.
You're going to come back with a book idea," my editor,
Katherine Jacobs, warned me. I assured her that writing was
the furthest thing from my mind.

Of course she was right. (She never gets tired of hearing
me say that.)

We'd started our honeymoon in gracefully chaotic Tokyo,

but made our way south, to the historic town of Tsumago in the Kiso Valley, along the old Nakasendo Highway that connected Tokyo to Kyoto. Tsumago became the first village to lead historic conservation efforts in Japan, and fought hard to protect its Edo-period (1600s–1868) buildings and traditions. All electrical lines and cables had to be buried; the village forbade any electric lighting along the streets. Our *ryokan*, the Fujioto, was nestled right in the heart of Tsumago's narrow streets along a winding mountainside with easy access to the historic highway, which we partially hiked on foot.

At nighttime, though, the village became something else entirely.

After a ten-course dinner of sashimi, boiled wasp larvae, *shabu-shabu*, green tea ice cream, and more, Jason and I decided to walk the foggy streets of Tsumago on Halloween night. Our only lighting was the dim halos of paper lanterns strung in front of the old houses. Each building loomed out of the mist like a secret. Even the moon stayed out of sight. The closer we drew to the town's center, the more certain we became that we were hearing something.

Drums. In the distance, we heard drummers, steady as a heartbeat, practicing through the night.

"You need to write a book about this," Jason said.

By the next morning when we toured the *waki-honjin* that served as Tsumago's historical museum, and saw the secret room where the villagers gathered to conspire against the shogunate, I knew the story I wanted to write.

To understand the tumultuous Edo period and its fraught transition into the Meiji era of openness, I turned to Marius B. Jansen's *The Making of Modern Japan* and Ryotara Shibu's *The Last Shogun: The Life of Tokugawa Yoshinobu*. Donald Keene's *World Within Walls: Japanese Literature of the Pre-modern Era—1600–1867* also provided invaluable cultural context about how Edo-period Japan viewed literature, stories, romance, and more, and informed Jiro's (and my) feeble attempts at Japanese-style poetry.

The Tokyo National Museum's online resources and the Samurai Archives research group were invaluable for the detailed descriptions of clothing, costumes, and more, while Emily Kubo's essays provided a fascinating and colorful history of Harajuku's weekly fashion display. Motohiso Yamakage's *The Essence of Shinto, Japan's Spiritual Heart* informed Kenji's interpretation of Shinto and the *kami*, though I acknowledge it is by no means authoritative. Finally, the heartbreaking and wonderful *Tale for the Time Being* by Ruth Ozeki offered a glimpse into modern Japanese culture, from *aidoru* to maid cafés and more, as well as further insight into the Buddhist mindset that underlies Japan in tandem with Shinto and many other traditions.

ACKNOWLEDGMENTS

REIKO AND MIYU TOOK A GREAT DEAL OUT OF ME, AND while this book was quick to draft, it was a real demon to whittle it down to its dark heart. I couldn't have survived it without the help of some incredible souls.

Katherine Jacobs at Roaring Brook Press, my enthusiastic editor, for whom no book idea is too weird and no "what if . . ." conversation too improbable. Elizabeth Clark, for yet another unbelievably gorgeous book cover.

Ammi-Joan Paquette, my indefatigable literary agent, giving me hope no matter how much I despair and giving my voice its space in the world.

Dahlia Adler, the best accountabilibuddy a soul could ask for, never tiring of my stressed-out, anxiety-riddled emails and always offering me a place to stay and loads of macarons every time I'm in New York.

Ellen Goodlett, whose notes on the first train wreck of this draft saved me endless heartache and who patiently corrected my god-awful *romaji*.

Katherine Locke, for guiding me patiently to the finish line and exorcising my fears; Misa Sugiura and Alyssa Furukawa, for their thoughtful critiques and discussions on representation; Emmy Neal, for catching all my mistakes in modern Japanese culture. Any remaining errors are my own.

My husband, Jason, without whom this book truly could not exist. I love you for so many reasons, but not least because I spent part of our honeymoon babbling about this ridiculous book idea, and you only encouraged me and came up with some twists of your own.

And finally, to the people of the wonderful town of Tsumago and the Fujioto *ryokan*. Thank you so much for inspiring Kuramagi, while still being nothing like the townsfolk in this book. Your hospitality and generosity are unmatched.